A huge wave suddenly swept over them

The suction of the receding water molded them together. Emma's eyes widened, and she gasped as she felt Rick's natural response to her body. Yet when she tried to pull back, the sand was drawn from under her feet, making her cling to him.

Her weight wasn't great, but the sand undermined his balance as well, toppling them both on the seabed.

Half drowning in seawater and warm, sensuous feeling, Emma could do nothing as Rick took her mouth again, pinning her body with his to keep her under him on the fine, shifting sand. He went on kissing her, his mouth hardening with desire that seemed reflected in the driving force of his limbs.

"Emma," he muttered. "Let me love you!"

MARGARET PARGETER
is also the author of these

Harlequin Presents

and these

Harlequin Romances

Many of these books are available at your local bookseller.

For a free catalog listing all titles currently available,
send your name and address to:

HARLEQUIN READER SERVICE
1440 South Priest Drive, Tempe, AZ 85281
Canadian address: Stratford, Ontario N5A 6W2

MARGARET PARGETER

substitute bride

Harlequin Books

TORONTO • NEW YORK • LOS ANGELES • LONDON
AMSTERDAM • PARIS • SYDNEY • HAMBURG
STOCKHOLM • ATHENS • TOKYO • MILAN

Harlequin Presents first edition March 1983
ISBN 0-373-10580-0

Original hardcover edition published in 1981
by Mills & Boon Limited

CHAPTER ONE

EMMA DAVIS smiled faintly as she turned to Jim Brown. 'You'd better get off home now, Jim, or Mary will be wondering what's happened to you.'

'If you're sure you can manage, Emma?'

'If I can't I'll send for you,' she promised, 'but it's not the first time I've managed on my own. Unless there are complications, I doubt if Daisy will need much help. After all,' Emma's young face softened wryly, 'this isn't exactly a new experience for her, is it?'

'No,' Jim conceded, as they both stood considering the cow who was expecting her fourth calf that evening, 'but you never know. The older I get the more I realise that even the most straightforward case can go wrong.'

Emma shrugged her slim shoulders, but didn't dismiss Jim's theory out of hand. No one knew better than herself just how wrong things could go on occasion. Very little on a farm ever went completely according to plan. The secret was to try and not worry over-much. 'I'll see you in the morning, Jim,' she said firmly.

After he had gone she sank down wearily on the old wooden stool beside Daisy, trying to ignore how tired she felt. It had been a long day and she couldn't see any immediate end to it. The farm wasn't large, but there was always plenty to do and she had only Jim to help her. A long day was endurable if it began at six and finished twelve hours later, but Emma's days rarely did. Even if all went well outside and she finished early there was usually plenty to do in the house. It was a relief, this evening, to know that both her aunt and cousin Blanche were out and she wouldn't have their dinner to cook. A snack on the end of the kitchen table for herself was all she need bother with.

A little happier because of this, Emma shifted her position on the stool, so she could lean against the wall of the barn and watch Daisy at the same time. Feeling more comfortable, she glanced down at the pair of old jeans she wore. They had been washed so often that they were too tight for real comfort and, like her shirt, were patched and worn. In a moment of raw retrospection, which she didn't usually allow herself, she wondered what her mother would have thought if she could have seen her now. Her mother had died many years ago, but Emma still remembered her delicate fastidiousness. Emma had been developing it herself to a lesser degree when her young life had been rudely shattered for the second time, when a trick of fate had caused her father's business to crash and brought on a heart attack from which he had never recovered.

The shock of this had been bad enough but there had been more to come. At sixteen she had had to leave her expensive boarding school to come and live here. Her uncle, her father's elder brother, had been kind to her, but compared with her lively, vital father he had seemed like an absentminded, tired old man. Never once had he appeared to notice how appallingly his wife and daughter treated Emma.

Immediately Emma arrived, they had persuaded him to dismiss the boy he employed and let Emma take his place. They had also made her do all the rough work in the house and most of the cooking. When her uncle had died a year later they had congratulated themselves that Emma was now quite competent to carry on alone.

That had been two years ago and Emma was still managing the farm alone, with only Jim to help her. She was quick and intelligent and didn't find this too difficult, especially as she had been so well taught by her uncle, but she hadn't wanted to make a career of it. It was simply because she was constantly reminded by her domineering aunt and cousin that she owed it to them to make the farm pay that she had agreed to stay and worked for nothing. She liked the farm, but she worried when things went wrong as so little money was put aside for emergencies. What there was to spare was usually spent immediately by Hilda and Blanche.

Emma sighed unhappily when she thought of her cousin. Blanche was twenty-five and beautiful, but very hard to please. She worked, on and off, as a model, but while she sometimes stayed in London when she had an assignment, she almost always tried to get home.

Two months ago Blanche had got herself engaged to a man called Richard Conway, who owned sugar plantations on the West Indian island of Barbados. They had met at a party and Richard, or Rick, as Blanche called him, had proposed the same week. Emma had only met him once, soon afterwards, when he had come to the farm, presumably to visit his future mother-in-law. He hadn't stayed long and Emma had only seen him for a few minutes, but what she had seen had surprised her. She had judged him to be about thirty-five or six and summed him up quickly, but without any real interest, as tall, dark and handsome. She hadn't liked his manner, which seemed as hard and domineering as her cousin's, which had made her decide disparagingly that they were well matched. Yet something about him had caught her attention, so that when her grey eyes had met his blue ones, for a few moments she had been unable to look away.

Later she dismissed the hurtful spark of sensitivity which shot through her as nonsense, guessing wryly that Richard Conway would be well versed in the ways of making women aware of him, even small, insignificant girls like herself. As he had been returning to Barbados almost immediately, she hadn't seen him again, but she had often wondered how a man like him could have fallen for someone as empty-headed as Blanche.

'He wants a wife,' Blanche, her face smug with self-satisfaction, had partly answered the question Emma dared not ask. She had just returned from seeing him off and was wearing a fabulous engagement ring. 'He fell for me at once.'

They had been alone and Emma stared at her. 'What are you going to do about Rex?' Rex Oliver and Blanche had been seeing quite a lot of each other and Emma was sure Blanche loved him as much as she was capable of loving anyone.

'Rex isn't the marrying kind,' Blanche had snapped, 'but then it's all right for a man. Rex will probably still be able to take his pick at forty, but my chances, both career-wise and matrimonial, can only get slimmer.'

'But I thought . . .' Emma began uncertainly, noticing that for all her contempt, when Rex was mentioned Blanche had gone pale.

'Well, you can stop thinking,' her cousin had advised sharply as Emma hesitated. 'I'm going to marry Rick, while I have the chance, and live on Barbados. I'm sick of living from hand to mouth in this dreary climate.'

'When are you getting married?' Emma had enquired curiously. 'Didn't he want to take you back with him? He doesn't look the sort to wait for anything he wants.'

'What would you know about what a man wants?' Blanche had sneered disparagingly. 'You've never even had a boy-friend! As a matter of fact Rick did ask me to go back with him but I don't like being rushed. I want a proper wedding, not a hole in the corner affair, and I had to have time to see Rex. I feel I owe it to him to say goodbye properly.'

As saying goodbye properly apparently meant seeing Rex each evening, Emma grew more and more confused.

Blanche's mother appeared to have no idea what was going on and Emma had no intention of enlightening her, but she couldn't help wondering what Richard Conway would say if he knew what his fiancée was up to. Rex Oliver, a wealthy night club proprietor, was without scruples when it came to getting his own way. He must be spending a small fortune on Blanche but, as Blanche said, had obviously no intention of settling down. Watching them together, in spite of her contempt, Emma couldn't help feeling anxious. In encouraging Rex, Blanche could easily be making a dreadful mistake, for if Richard found out, Emma suspected he would never forgive her.

Blanche might be lucky, of course, she usually was. People often excused her because she was beautiful. Because of her beauty she was able to get away with little short of murder. When Emma considered her own plainness she was amazed that two cousins could be so different. Blanche had, according to her mother, taken after her side of the family for looks, yet Emma could remember her own mother being quite pretty and her father had been handsome. Emma's mirror reflected none of the attractiveness Blanche had inherited. She saw only a slightly tilted nose set in an ordinary face above a mouth which curved too generously. Her mane of fair hair, when properly groomed, might be her one saving grace. Once she had thought it might be her figure, but all the work involved in completing the spring sowing had reduced her delicate slenderness to a bony thinness, and her usual curves, which she had once been told by a rather precocious school friend would soon have men chasing her, were now almost non-existent.

'Hello there!'

Hearing the voice of the man she had just been thinking of, so unexpectedly, Emma almost jumped out of her skin. As she stumbled to her feet, her small face flushed scarlet, then went pale as she turned towards the door.

'Mr Conway!' she gasped breathlessly, 'you gave me an awful fright!'

'If you hadn't been daydreaming you would have heard me coming,' he smiled. 'And the name's Rick.'

'Yes,' she contrived to recover her breath, 'but I didn't know you were due. When did you get back?'

'I flew in this afternoon.' Quietly he stepped inside the barn and closed the door. 'I couldn't find anyone at the house. Is everyone out, apart from you?'

Cautiously Emma lowered her long, thick lashes to hide her sudden dismay. 'Yes,' she said.

His impatient sigh reached her. 'Just my luck. You'd better tell me where Blanche is.'

This time Emma had to swallow. 'I believe she's working, but don't ask me where. You should have let her know you were coming.'

'Perhaps,' his enigmatic glance pierced her. 'So you've no idea where she can be found?'

Awkwardly, Emma paused, knowing she could never tell him his fiancée was out with another man. For one thing, Rick Conway, whom she had only met once before, made her nervous enough when he was pleasant. She couldn't imagine how she would feel if he flew into a temper, which he seemed more than capable of doing. And for another, she hated hurting people, and even a man as tough and cynical as Rick appeared to be, might be capable of feeling hurt. Judging him, from their brief acquaintance, she doubted it, but he must have some normal feelings to have got himself engaged. She would take a lot of convincing that loving a girl was one of them, but there was something about his mouth which suggested strong passions. Unhappily, aware that he was waiting, Emma shook her head at his question, suddenly horrified that he might be thinking of remaining here until Blanche returned.

'I'm in no hurry,' he smiled, confirming her worst fears,

as he glanced at his watch. 'I was passing through, so to speak, and decided to surprise her. As often happens,' he added dryly, 'the surprise hasn't quite worked out. Are you sure she didn't say where she was working, then I could go and pick her up?'

Emma's grey eyes widened apprehensively as they met probing dark blue ones. Fortunately Daisy gave a kind of agonised, uneasy grunt which drew their attention. It soon became apparent that Daisy's grunt didn't mean something was about to happen immediately, but it did give Emma breathing space.

'I'm afraid I don't always ask where she's working,' she replied evasively. 'She might have said, but if she did I must have had too much on my mind to take it in.'

'I see.' As if accepting this at last, he crossed the width of the barn to pause by Emma's side. As she hastily resumed her seat, he stood staring down at her. 'There seems nothing I can do now but wait.'

The barn was growing darker, as night fell, but was quite cosy and warm. Strangely, Emma felt the odd sense of intimacy again, exactly as she had felt the first time he had looked at her. Uneasily she glanced away from him, wishing he wasn't so aggressively masculine. Having come straight from the airport, he was wearing the same grey suit he had travelled in and the darkness of his tan was emphasised by the pristine whiteness of his thin silk shirt. She was vitally aware of his strongly defined features and tall, leanly muscled frame. Something inside her tightened almost painfully, only relaxing when he turned his attention to Daisy again.

'Don't you have a man around to deal with this kind of thing?' he frowned.

Emma smiled, showing small, perfect teeth. 'Daisy won't need much help, and I'm used to it.'

'I still think you should call in your manager,' he said shortly. 'It's no job for a girl.'

'We don't have a manager,' she explained. 'There's only old Jim.'

'But I thought——' Rick's dark brows furrowed, then he shrugged. 'I must have misunderstood something Blanche said. I assumed you had plenty of help.'

The derisive amusement which fleetingly flickered over Emma's face didn't escape him. 'Why do you look like that?' he asked sharply.

'Like what?' She was genuinely puzzled.

His mouth clamped impatiently as he obviously thought her intentionally devious. 'I seem to sense a certain criticism of your cousin. I suppose it could be that you're jealous of her?'

'Jealous?' Emma jumped to her feet again, her face flushing indignantly.

With a sardonic smile on his lips, he studied her coolly. 'You must have noticed that Blanche is beautiful, while you are plain.'

Emma's flush deepened painfully, but when she tried to retaliate a sudden, inexplicable flood of tears threatened to choke her.

Seeing them running down her cheeks, Rick Conway exclaimed tersely, 'I'm sorry—that was inexcusable and cruel of me. I often forget how sensitive women are, but for God's sake don't cry. The truth seldom hurts anyone.'

Hastily, feeling utterly humiliated by her own unaccountable weakness, Emma accepted his clean white handkerchief. 'Please take no notice,' she whispered stiffly. 'It wasn't so much what you said. Believe me, I've no illusions about my looks. You must have caught me at a vulnerable moment. We've been busy lately and I must be overtired.'

'And I haven't exactly helped,' he commented dryly. 'I ought to have let Blanche know I was coming. If I had you would at least have been spared this.'

'It doesn't really matter,' Emma insisted, her thoughts

too busy now to allow for sulks. She could see he wasn't going to change his mind about staying, and she wondered uneasily what time Blanche would be back. Hadn't she said something about Rex bringing her home, so she could change before they went on to dance somewhere? Casting a furtive glance at Rick, as she returned his handkerchief, Emma realised she must somehow get rid of him before then.

'Wouldn't it be better if you returned to London and called to see Blanche tomorrow?' she suggested hopefully.

He merely smiled and shook his head. 'I'm in no hurry,' he drawled, 'I'll wait.'

Emma tried again. 'She could be staying in town?'

'No, I checked her flat. Her roommate said she was coming here.'

'You might get tired of waiting.'

Rick's smile was faint and wry. 'Don't you think it might be worth it? It's quite a time since I had a woman in my arms. If a man has a conscience, being engaged rather limits his activities in that direction, if his fiancée isn't around.' Tauntingly, his eyes glinted on Emma's closed face. 'I don't suppose you know much about that kind of deisre, little Miss Davis?'

Again Emma flushed, with a mixture of anger and embarrassment. 'I'm not as ignorant as all that!' she lied definatly. 'I do have boy-friends.'

'I wonder?' he mused softly, his dark brows rising, slightly insolent as his glance wandered consideringly around the cowshed. 'I suppose this kind of thing does tend to rub off eventually?'

'You're still being insulting!" she retorted sharply.

'I didn't mean to be,' he shrugged. 'I believe any man would prefer a little earthiness to ice. Come to think of it,' his blue eyes were suddenly keener, 'you have a very promising mouth. With a little tuition,' he grinned, 'of the right kind, you might have distinct possibilities.'

'Which I suppose,' she snapped, 'might make up for my lack of beauty?'

'Well, no one,' he taunted, 'needs rose-coloured spectacles in bed.'

His careless frankness was making her quiver and bringing wild colour to her pale cheeks. Yet there was nothing really offensive in his manner. He was annoyed because Blanche wasn't here and was obviously getting rid of his frustration. Rex Oliver often said much the same kind of thing, but the effect was different. Some of his remarks to Blanche made Emma almost squirm. Often she felt like telling him to shut up, only Blanche wouldn't have thanked her. Frankly, she didn't know how Blanche could stand him, especially now she was engaged to a man like Rick Conway.

'Are you in England for long?' she made a rather obvious attempt to change the conversation.

'Just for the next couple of days,' he replied, surprising her. 'This is why I feel it's important to see Blanche tonight. I have to fly to Australia for approximately three weeks. My cousin runs some sugar plantations in Northern Queensland for me and something has come up unexpectedly. I could have taken Blanche with me and made it part of our honeymoon, but there'll be a lot of business to get through and not much time for pleasure. Somehow I couldn't see her enjoying it. I thought three weeks would give her time to complete her preparations for our wedding and we could be married immediately I got back.'

'That seems reasonable.' Emma, realising her own voice sounded remarkably flat, tried to smile to make up for it.

'I already have a licence,' he said lightly. 'Think she'll be pleased?'

'Of course.' Again Emma was aware of a curious hollowness inside her and wondered why it was there. Surely she didn't imagine she was going to miss having Blanche around? Yet what else could it be? Bewildered, she raised confused eyes to meet Rick Conway's and, once more, found herself caught in a moment of peculiar tension.

Again she had a feeling that something momentous had been avoided when Daisy gave another roar of indignant pain, as the calf within her stirred. Quickly Emma went down on her knees in the straw, speaking to her softly while she gently soothed the animal's hot neck with her small hand. 'Rick . . .' she began.

'Emma,' swiftly he drew her to her feet, after glancing at Daisy with quick comprehension, 'I'm hungry. It must be hours since I've eaten. Why not go and make us both something while I keep watch here?'

'But she looks . . .' Anxiously, Emma stared down over her shoulder as Rick held her, trying to decide exactly how Daisy looked. 'I don't want anything to go wrong,' she frowned, moving uneasily away from him. 'If anything was to happen while . . .'

'Nothing's going to happen while you're gone,' he let her go mockingly, 'I'll be here. My interests lie mainly in sugar, but I've managed horses and stock all my life.'

'Well, if you're sure?' Daisy seemed to be reproaching her with huge, soft brown eyes, but Rick was so adamant he was leaving Emma with little choice. Wearily, the fight momentarily going out of her, she bent her fair head. 'I admit I would love a cup of tea, but you must promise you'll come for me if anything happens.'

'I'll let you know if anything goes wrong,' he promised, with a deviousness she didn't think about until afterwards.

In the house, in the small kitchen, as she swiftly cooked a light meal, Emma thought wistfully how nice it was to have a pair of broad shoulders to lean on, if only figuratively. Blanche was a fool to run the risks she did, and the sooner she realised it the better. By continuing to go out with Rex Oliver she was playing with fire, and while Emma felt she hated Rick Conway after the disparaging remarks he had made about her looks, she sensed he was twice the man Rex would ever be.

Some might say Blanche deserved to lose her fiancé, but Emma found it hard to be vindictive. She had tried to warn Blanche, as soon as she had come into the house, but had been unable to get hold of her. She had even tried to ring Rex at two of his clubs. She had gone to a lot of trouble finding the numbers, but had been no more successful with him, either. Now she could only hope that Blanche would see Rick's hired car and send Rex away before it was too late. Sometimes Blanche appeared to have the intuition of an alley cat, and Emma prayed that, on this occasion, it wouldn't let her down.

Leaving a pan of soup simmering on the hotplate, she went to tell Rick that dinner was ready and was surprised to find Jim Brown in the barn with him.

'We were both present at the birth,' Rick said solemnly, as Emma's eyes widened with dismay, 'so there's no need to worry.'

Daisy, a proud mother, was giving all her attention to her newly born calf. Emma, her small face lighting with a gentle tenderness, watched them until Rick, his eyes fixed curiously on her, reminded her dryly that he was still hungry.

'Oh, I'm sorry,' she flushed, 'that's what I came to tell you about. I have something waiting.' Jumping up from her crouched position beside Daisy, she smiled warmly at Jim, who said he could manage now, and there was no need for her to come back.

'I hope you didn't ruin your suit.' Suddenly remembering he wasn't exactly dressed for the kind of work he had been doing, she glanced at Rick anxiously as they entered the kitchen.

'I found some old waterproofs hanging behind a door,' he assured her. 'Not that it mattered. I have another suit in the car and could always have got something in London tomorrow.'

'How nice to have plenty of money!' she retorted sharply, before quite realising what she was saying.

'Waspish tongues often go with plain faces,' he observed indifferently.

He watched with unrepentant satisfaction as she went scarlet, and she knew intuitively that he enjoyed hurting her. She sensed, swiftly appalled, that given the opportunity he would take a sadistic pleasure in it. The awareness between them, if he was conscious of it at all, wasn't something he was going to let her enjoy!

'When you've quite finished insulting me,' she snapped, 'I'll show you where you can wash your hands—unless you remember?'

'The kitchen sink will do,' he said, and proceeded to use it, after taking off his jacket and shirt.

Open-mouthed, her throat curiously dry, Emma watched as he turned on the taps before reaching for the soap. His back was broad and when he twisted slightly sideways, she saw the crisp curling hair which covered his strongly muscled chest. Hastily, as he finished rinsing the faint bloodstains from his arms and began drying them, she turned away. Trying to steady her breath, she began ladling soup into the golden earthenware bowls on the table.

She didn't look at him as he sat down, hating the peculiar heat which seemed to be surging right through her. Impatiently she wondered what was wrong with her and wished her hands would stop trembling.

'That was good.' She winced at Rick Conway's sigh of pleasure as she removed his empty bowl. 'Did you make it?'

'Yes,' she set the main course before him with a flat little frown, 'I prepared it last night, after I finished outside, before I went to bed. I'm glad you enjoyed it.'

His brows lifted as though he was impressed, as he glanced up at her. 'You're a good cook. This steak is delicious, too. I don't think I've tasted better.'

'It's not the best.' Emma wondered why she was bothering to explain, unless it was because praise was so unknown to her she was letting it go to her head. 'But I prepare it well beforehand, too, for the best results.' Her sense of humour suddenly reasserting itself, she grinned, 'I do have some redeeming features, you see.'

Rick's eyebrows quirked again, but he said nothing, and her smile faded as she bitterly rebuked herself for fishing for compliments. Her face going quite pale, she looked away, staring blindly down at her own piece of steak, which she suddenly didn't feel like eating.

'Do you often eat out?' He sighed, as if, noting her despondency, he was searching for a topic to amuse her.

'Me? Oh,' she smiled again, wryly, 'almost never.'

'When Blanche and I are married you'll have to come and stay with us,' he said formally. 'I think you would enjoy our West Indian food.'

'Yes, possibly.' Her reply sounded stilted, she knew, but she couldn't find anything else to say. After Rick Conway married she wasn't sure that she'd be wise to see more of him than was necessary. They didn't get on.

'Shall I make coffee?' he offered unexpectedly. 'I can see you're tired.'

Because she couldn't recall anyone suggesting she was tired since she came here, she blinked in astonishment. 'If you like,' she indicated the percolator on the sink. 'I'm not all that tired, though, and when Blanche comes I'll go to bed.'

He filled the percolator before he enquired thoughtfully, 'How much land do you have here?'

'Just over a hundred acres. And you?' she asked, hoping to divert him.

He smiled, as if her blunt question amused him. 'Considerably more than that, I'm afraid.'

Emma noticed he didn't reveal anything. 'I suppose I

ought to thank you for helping this evening.'

'Not if you don't feel like it,' he returned tauntingly.

It was an effort to meet the dark eyes, which Emma sensed were watching her cynically. 'You seemed to think nothing of it.'

'I'm quite good with human babies as well,' he assured her lightly. 'On a sugar plantation things can happen very quickly and there isn't always time to fetch a doctor.'

Was he deliberately trying to embarrass her? Her cheeks pink, Emma suspected he was, and her fingers curled tightly. 'You must be looking forward to having a son of your own,' she remarked stiffly.

'First priority,' he agreed coldly.

'You sound as if you were providing a part for a business machine!' she accused him. 'Babies need love.'

'Should be born out of love, is what you're trying to say, isn't it?' His eyes were hard. 'We aren't all romantic idealists, Emma, but supposing you look after your affairs and allow me to look after mine?'

'I think . . .' Emma was beginning hotly, when the hall door suddenly burst open and to her horrified consternation Blanche rushed into the kitchen, closely followed by Rex Oliver.

Emma felt like sinking through the floor. If she hadn't been so busy quarrelling with Rick she might have heard Blanche come in. Her face so pale as to cause Rick Conway to glance at her sharply, she stumbled to her feet. Desperately she tried to utter a word of warning, but only an odd croaking sound fell from her frozen lips.

It amazed her, afterwards, to realise she needn't have worried. Blanche, with her usual cunning, took care of the situation immediately, after a mere flicker of stunned surprise. As Rick stepped forward, she launched herself straight at him with a shrill cry. 'Rick! Oh, darling, isn't this wonderful!'

Numbly Emma watched as his arms went around her

and his head lowered in a brief but warm kiss. 'I was beginning to think you were never coming,' he grumbled lightly, yet there was nothing indulgent in his eyes as they went speculatively over the man she had arrived with.

Blanche sounded quite breathless, as if Rick's kiss had lasted longer than it had. Her eyes glittered too, but with a peculiar kind of excitement. 'It's wonderful to see you,' she repeated, 'but you should have let me know you were coming. I might not have been here yet if I hadn't remembered that Rex was taking Emma out this evening and rang him to beg a lift home.' With a charming smile she glanced at Emma. 'Rex kept grumbling that I'd made him late, but I told him you'd probably have forgotten, anyway. Am I right?'

As Emma tried desperately to pull herself together, Blanche gracefully contrived to turn her back on Rick, to stare meaningfully from Rex to Emma.

Rex was the first to catch on, perhaps because in his line of business he was used to dealing with unusual situations and had to keep his wits about him. With a charming smile he caught Emma to him, lightly kissing her bewildered lips. 'I can see you've been busy, darling, so it maybe doesn't matter that I'm late, but if we're going dancing you'd better get a move on.'

'Dancing?' she whispered, her grey eyes round as she tried unhappily to wriggle from his arms.

'Don't tell me you really had forgotten?' he teased, while his fingers dug cruelly in her arm, like a warning. She heard him take a deep breath as he glanced at Rick Conway. 'Emma gets so absorbed in the farm she often forgets about me.'

'We may as well all go dancing,' Blanche said quickly, as something about Emma's expression convinced her that her schemes could still go awry. 'Can't we, darling?' brightly she appealed to a silent Rick.

'Anything you like,' he agreed lazily, as she slipped a

loving hand through his arm, 'but we do have a lot to discuss.'

Blanche frowned. 'Surely nothing that can't wait?'

'We have a wedding to arrange,' he replied lightly. 'Ours.' He took no notice of the others.

'Wedding?' Blanche looked startled, almost shocked.

'We are engaged, remember?' Rick reminded her, very dryly.

'Yes, of course.' Blanche's smile, Emma saw, was very pleasant, if a trifle forced. As she watched, Blanche's mouth drooped petulantly. 'I hadn't forgotten, Rick, but you might have let me know you were coming. I can't just drop everything at a moment's notice. I have my modelling contracts to fulfil.'

Rick's eyes narrowed, then he shrugged. 'We can't talk about this here,' he flicked an enigmatic glance at Rex which again betrayed no immediate liking for what he saw. 'Perhaps later.'

There was dislike on Rick Conway's face but no real suspicion. With an air of lazy amusement the arm Rex had placed around Emma tightened. She could sense the almost bizarre pleasure he was deriving from her discomfort, felt it increase when he urged her softly to hurry up and change. 'If you're feeling exhausted, darling, I can always come and help,' he grinned, adding outrageously, 'It wouldn't be the first time.'

'I can manage,' she murmured, restraining an urgent desire to slap his leering face. Meeting the brief anger in Rick Conway's, she felt sickened. It wasn't hard to guess what he was thinking. Blanche had a lot to answer for, but for once she might have bitten off more than she could chew. She would need brains as well as her normal cunning to find her way successfully through this little lot! Surely she didn't expect her to actually go dancing with them? She couldn't have forgotten Emma hadn't a thing to wear.

Yet for all she felt she despised her, it was for Blanche's sake that Emma found herself nodding stiffly at Rex. 'Just give me a few minutes. I'm afraid I've——' pausing, she cast an apologetic glance towards Rick, 'I mean, we've been busy, and I forgot about everything else.' Trying to control a note of sheer fright in her voice, she turned to Blanche. 'You'll be coming up to change, too, won't you, before we go?'

'After I take Rex and Rick into the lounge and find them something decent to drink.' She tossed a distasteful glance at the now cold coffee. 'You go ahead.'

When Blanche followed her a little later, Emma was sitting on the edge of her bed. She stared at Blanche, who was looking unbelievably pleased with herself.

'What do we do now?' she asked, her own face white.

'Do?' Blanche smiled, a gleeful little smile as she threw off her coat, as if the two men downstairs presented no great problem. 'Hope for the best, I suppose,' she replied, with a coolness Emma found it difficult to emulate.

'I think you're acting deplorably, going out with one man while you're engaged to another!' she suddenly found the courage to say furiously.

'Now don't go getting all steamed up!' Blanche advised nastily. 'How was I to know Rick would arrive? If you'd had any sense, you would have contrived to get me word he was here and all this might have been avoided.' Her pale blues eyes cold with dislike, she snapped at Emma spitefully, 'You're so bloody self-righteous I expect you prayed the worst might happen so you could say I told you so!'

CHAPTER TWO

IN the quiet of the bedroom nothing could be heard but the sound of Blanche's viciously drawn breath. Emma, taking a quick glance at her, swallowed nervously. Blanche's language didn't frighten her so much as the hatred in her voice. Blanche was making no attempt to disguise the fact that she despised her.

Biting her lip on an unhappy sigh, Emma managed a rather muddled dignity. 'I did try to ring, but no one seemed to know where I could find you. And if Rick did break off the engagement you would only have yourself to blame, and I certainly wouldn't waste my time saying I told you so.'

It was the nearest Emma had come to defying the other girl, and the effort proved almost too much for her. Twin patches of colour tinted her pale cheeks and her voice trembled.

Blanche, apparently fearing she was going to have a case of hysteria on her hands, said quickly, 'I'm sorry. I agree you have a point, but you can't let me down now. You've got to help me!'

Emma could almost see the way her mind was working. Blanche wouldn't have spared her another word, at least not a civil one, if it hadn't been for the two men downstairs 'If helping you means going out tonight, I'm afraid I can't.'

'It's not much to ask, darling,' Blanche was shamelessly wheedling now. 'We'll go somewhere quiet, where Rex and I aren't known, and only stay an hour or two.'

'What it boils down to,' said Emma, recovering some of her poise, 'is that you're asking me to help deceive Rick. That's what I don't like, for a start.'

'What can it mean to you?' Blanche's face was almost ugly as her temper rose again. 'Don't tell me,' she sneered, 'that you've fallen for him!'

'Hardly.' Emma's soft mouth twisted ironically. 'What chance do you think I would stand with a man like that? But,' she attacked her cousin fiercely, 'if I had fallen for him and felt like encouraging him, I hope I'd have had the decency to remember there are such things as principles and loyalty. If Rick knew what was going on I'm sure he wouldn't want anything more to do with you.'

'How do you know?' Blanche retaliated contemptuously. 'Do you imagine he's any saint himself? I don't see why, if I have to overlook his affairs, he shouldn't do the same where I'm concerned. Why should different rules apply for men and women?'

'Just as long as you realise what you're doing,' Emma sighed tersely, suddenly realising it was a waste of time trying to make Blanche see sense.

'We've been through all this before, Emma,' Blanche pleaded, after an uneasy pause during which she made an almost visible attempt to control her angry impatience. Her voice harsh with effort, she begged, 'Please, just put on a dress and stop arguing.'

'I don't have a dress.'

'What?' Emma might have dropped a bomb without its effect being so shattering. Blanche's fury increased as she believed Emma was being deliberately obstructive. 'When you came here you had several,' she exclaimed. 'Any one of them will do.'

Scornfully Emma lifted her chin. 'Your mother took them. I didn't ask what she did with them. I only have one, which she didn't think was worth bothering about. It was one I had at school for some event, if I remember, when I was fourteen.'

Blanche had the grace to colour, but there was no apology in her voice as she snapped, 'They were ridicu-

lously expensive models from Paris—what good would
they have been to you here? The moths would only have
got into them, and you cost us quite a lot of money, one
way and another. It was the only way we could get any of
it back.'

'It doesn't matter now,' Emma assured her briefly,
indeed finding it almost impossible to believe she had once
owned quite a few evening gowns, each worth many hundreds of pounds. In some things her father had always
spoiled her, perhaps because he had liked showing her off.
All his possessions had had to measure up to a certain
standard, his daughter included, young though she had
been.

As no amount of retrospection would solve tonight's
problem, Emma sighed and pushed it to the back of her
mind. 'You could let me borrow one of your dresses,' she
suggested to an angry, frowning Blanche.

'Mine wouldn't be much good,' Blanche glared at her,
'except for a laugh. I'm much taller than you, you'd only
look silly, and you look bad enough as it is. No, you'd
better wear your old one, if you can find it.'

'Won't you mind if I look even worse than usual?'
Emma asked dryly.

'Who's going to notice you when I'm around?' Blanche
snapped derisively.

It wasn't until later that Emma realised how true this
was. No one had noticed. Swallowing to relieve a surprising tightness in her throat, she tried to relax in Rex
Oliver's arms as they circled the dance floor of the night
club they had found. As she had walked downstairs,
covered from chin to toe in prim grey sateen, to join the
others in the hall, if there had been anything in Rick
Conway's eyes it had only been a faint amusement. It
had been painfully obvious that outdated styles and a
profusion of fair hair tied hastily back from an even more
hastily powdered face left him quite indifferent.

As it was the first opportunity she had had of speaking to Rex alone, she was determined to make the most of it. 'Why do you keep on seeing Blanche, Rex? You know she's engaged.'

Rex groaned lightly, glancing down into her indignant eyes with a hint of disappointment on his good-looking but rather weak face. 'Don't spoil it, Emma!'

'Spoil what?'

'Well,' he grinned suddenly, 'you may be a plain little thing, but you dance like an angel. For your dancing alone I could love you.'

'Stop being so silly and evasive, Rex!' She could have stamped her small foot that he wasn't apparently inclined to take her seriously.

Again his mouth twitched, then he sobered, his eyes narrowing as he studied her upturned features. 'Do you know,' he frowned, 'I do believe you have distinct possibilities.'

'Oh, for goodness' sake, Rex, we're not discussing me! Besides, what you suggest is ridiculous. I expect,' she stared at him almost belligerently, 'you're just trying to put me off.'

'No,' adamantly he shook his head as he went on studying her, 'I'm too used to assessing raw material, if you'll forgive the pun, to dismiss you out of hand. I'm suddenly convinced I could turn you into something outstanding. If you ever need a job, Emma . . .'

'I don't,' she cut through what looked like becoming a definite offer, abruptly, wondering why men liked to tease when something important was at stake. 'We're talking about Blanche.'

'You are,' he corrected smoothly. 'You've implied that I'm corrupting an innocent young girl. Well, let's get one thing straight. True, Blanche is engaged, but she is neither innocent or a young girl like you any more. She stopped being either years ago.'

'But all that's behind her now,' Emma insisted hollowly. 'She's going to settle down, I'm sure of it. And she'll have Rick to help her.'

'Oh, Conway doesn't mind her the way she is. I'm not saying she isn't delectable, but in another year or two, when the glamour wears off, what will he be left with?'

Emma shivered as she recognised the truth of this. In the mornings, Blanche with a hangover and without make-up could easily pass for a woman years older. 'That's not the point, though, is it?' She wasn't sure whether she was arguing with herself or Rex, but there had to be some way out of what she sensed was impending disaster.

'Never mind about the point, child,' Rex's arms tightened irritably. 'Blanche is quite capable of sorting out her own problems, and I never interfere unless I'm asked.'

That was part of the trouble! Everyone, including Blanche, thought she was more than capable of taking care of herself, but was she? Wasn't there such a thing as having too much faith in one's own infallibility? No one appeared to realise Blanche could need help, and here was Rex, who Emma was certain Blanche might listen to, refusing to even consider giving it!

Unhappily Emma's eyes wandered to where Blanche was dancing with Rick Conway. She appeared to have made an extra effort this evening and her appearance was scintillating. So was her dress—what there was of it! As she watched broodingly, Emma's eyes widened as she saw Rick's hand caressing Blanche's waist, which the low back of her dress left bare, then, to her disgust, he drew Blanche even closer and his hand slid upwards into the brief bodice, where Emma considered no man's hand had a right to be.

Suddenly, as if he sensed an audience, Rick's eyes lifted from the sophisticated girl in his arms to meet the open scorn in Emma's directly. As she flushed but was unable to look away, his mouth curled contemptuously. 'Yes, take a good look,' his mocking expression seemed to say, 'No man's going to admire you enough to want to possess you.'

Feeling utterly humiliated by a message she received only too clearly, Emma almost refused to dance with him when he asked her later. And though she sensed his surprised pleasure in the perfect unison of their limbs she hated him too much to forgive him. He didn't talk much, but he did ask if she had known Rex Oliver long.

'Quite a long time,' she replied cautiously, trying in vain to remember when it was that Blanche had first brought Rex to the house.

'Are you sure's he's your type?' Rick continued bluntly. 'Now wait a minute!' he threw up a quick hand as Emma started and stared at him resentfully. 'So far as I can make out you've no one to advise you. Or perhaps I should forget about trying to be diplomatic? Blanche was just saying how you won't listen to advice.'

'Why, of all—all the . . .'

'You wouldn't be prepared to listen to me either, I suppose?' he asked coldly, ignoring her outburst which had petered out in such a way as seemed to proclaim her guilt.

'Why should I listen to you, or anyone?' Emma drew a deep breath, her voice icy. 'Give me one good reason!'

'Why, indeed?' Suddenly his mouth relaxed in faint irony. 'Apart from giving you a hand with Daisy, I haven't done much to endear myself to you, have I? I waded in with a heavy hand regarding your appearance, putting your back up immediately. I guess I forgot I wasn't talking to my young sister.'

'I don't think you did.' Emma felt a tremor run through her as his arms tightened unpredictably at that.

'Astute, as well as a good cook and an astonishingly good dancer,' he quirked, 'to say nothing of being a competent farmer. Perhaps if you were to advertise your talents more, a man wouldn't notice—other things?'

'Strangers don't usually wade in with insults,' she retorted coldly, refusing to be impressed by a few flattering words—if that was what they had been.

'That's not how I'd have described a few straight remarks,' he drawled. 'And I can hardly be classed as a stranger.'

'We'd only met once,' she exclaimed.

'Perhaps that was where I made my first mistake. I should have made more of that opportunity, but you didn't give me much encouragement. You just stood and stared at me out of those great condemning eyes and disliked me on sight.'

'How could I do that?' Was she asking him or herself? 'I didn't even know you. I do recall wondering why you'd chosen Blanche—I mean, after all the other girls you must have met nearer home.'

'Maybe none of them would have me.'

'We both know that couldn't be true.'

His eyebrows rose so sardonically she flushed. 'Don't tell me you think me handsome enough to attract any number of women?' he teased, with a sober insolence which somehow got under her skin.

'Perhaps it's your bank balance more than you,' she replied stiffly, but felt a flicker of triumphant malice as she saw his mouth tighten. When it came down to it, Rick Conway would enjoy being married for what he had no more than the next man.

He was about to speak when the music stopped, and Emma was relieved, as she guessed the nature of the few terse words he had been about to deliver. She was glad he wasn't given another chance to reprimand her as Blanche and Rex happened to be beside them.

Rex claimed Emma for nearly every dance after that, and for all she disliked him she began to enjoy herself.

Never having danced since she left school, she hadn't realised how much she had missed it.

Rex, strangely enough, was enjoying himself, too, and as he and Emma sparred lightly the habitual boredom seemed to leave his face. Once, when Emma said something which amused him greatly, he laughed aloud and hugged her appreciatively to him. She was aware that Rick had noticed and, as before, didn't conceal his contempt. Blanche frowned, as she and Rick danced past, not bothering to hide hers, either, as she saw Rex's amusement.

Later, when she and Blanche were in the cloakroom together, Blanche insisted that there was no need for Emma to overdo things.

The grey dress was so cumbersome and hot, Emma was having to hold her thin wrists under the cold tap to try and cool down. When Blanche spoke she stared at her blankly. 'I thought you wanted me to pretend Rex is my boy-friend?'

'All right, so I did,' Blanche snapped, 'but I didn't ask you to go as far as you're going!'

Soon afterwards they left to return to the farm, where both Rex and Rick departed within minutes of each other. To Emma's surprise Rick went first, but he did arrange to return the following evening to finalise plans with Blanche.

The whole of the next day went with unusual slowness for Emma. Everything dragged, and whereas before there had never seemed to be enough time, now there was too much. It maddened her, too, that she couldn't stop thinking of Rick Conway. Why was it, when she had danced with him, she had experienced those strange sensations again? It must have something to do with the antagonism they felt towards each other. It could be nothing else. A girl might be well advised not to trust him, though. Emma shivered when she recalled the dark look in his eyes when she had defied him and the curious cruelty around his sensuous mouth as his glance had flickered over hers.

As Rick was taking Blanche out to dinner and Aunt Hilda was dining out again with friends, Emma decided she would wait until they had all gone and enjoy the luxury of a bath instead of making do with a shower. For once she had managed to finish early and was busy washing the dishes which were still in the sink from lunch, when she heard the doorbell ring. Fancying that no one had answered it, she hastily removed the last of the dishes from the soapy water and quickly dried her wet hands.

Flinging open the kitchen door, she was startled and embarrassed to find Rick Conway slowly removing his mouth from Blanche's, in what had obviously been a very pleasurable kiss. He had his arms about her and was kissing her in a lazy, teasing fashion, while again his hands caressed her bare back. Emma gulped, feeling her face go red. No man had ever touched her like that. There was something very intimate in the way Rick's fingers were moving over bare flesh. What did he think he was doing?

Her cheeks so hot she could scarcely bear them, Emma hid her punishing discomposure beneath scorn, letting it show clearly in her cool grey eyes as they clashed with Rick's.

Lifting his head, he met Emma's silent disgust head on. Anger flared for an instant in the darkness of his face and his hands tightened until Blanche, not realising the cause of it, squealed in protest.

Without waiting to say hello, Emma turned quickly, stumbling back into the kitchen. As she did so she heard Blanche say coldly that she didn't like being mauled and would go upstairs and fetch a coat.

Emma, feeling irrationally like someone who had ran a great distance and was quite out of breath, was about to collapse weakly on to a chair when the door behind her snapped open and two hands yanked her ruthlessly to her feet. Swiftly she was turned to face the man who held her. 'Don't ever look at me like that again, young lady!' Rick snarled, pulling her without warning towards him.

She saw his mouth swooping downwards, but could do nothing to avoid it. It took her unawares and her last breath away with it. His hold on her was savage, renewing her former suspicions that he enjoyed hurting her, but this time he used actions as well as words, which hurt even more. Although his hands didn't stray his mouth did. She could have sworn that for all his ferocious beginning he had meant to treat her lightly, but when he drew back, after touching her lips briefly, his mouth suddenly descended again, this time to crush hers relentlessly.

Instinctively, as molten flames began pouring through her, she tried to push him away, but his arms merely tightened about her, putting a decisive end to her struggles. She could feel the heat emanating from him and her whole body went limp with shock, yet when she put her hands up to push him away, she found them clinging instead to the hard strength of his broad shoulders. His voice was deep as he muttered incomprehensibly against her throbbing lips, and she felt her senses flare with what she refused to acknowledge as something very like desire. Shuddering beneath his brutal expertise, she tried to stop thinking, but as his determined assault continued her fair head was bent back, until she feared her slender neck might break before he released her.

For a long, hateful moment, when he did, they stared at each other, and she saw his eyes had changed and darkened while his breath came harshly.

'A man's hands are rather tied when it comes to punishing a woman,' he said curtly, 'but you asked for that.'

'No, I didn't!' Regaining a little composure, she hit back. 'I didn't like the way you were pawing Blanche and

I wasn't going to pretend that I did!'

'My God!' his eyes were hard and scornful, 'you're a fine one to talk! You're scarcely in any position to sit in judgment on me. Your friend Rex Oliver told me too much last night, while you and Blanche were upstairs getting ready.'

'You talked about me?' Emma's blood ran cold. 'You had a nerve!'

'It wasn't exactly me who did the talking,' Rick snapped, 'it was your boy-friend, your lover, the man you want to marry but who is—and he swears you know it—trying to shake you off. Hence the reason why he was deliberately late last night. It had nothing to do with Blanche.'

Emma felt her cheeks grow white. 'Rex didn't? He couldn't say that!'

'Oh, come off it, Emma. No need to look so horrified. You're no innocent virgin and could be older than you look. I've been enlightened. There's no need to put on an act for me. Poor Blanche, no wonder she's been trying to save you from yourself. Rex, I believe, hasn't been the only man.'

Emma stared and winced. She could do nothing else, yet was puzzled that she didn't denounce Rex and Blanche right away. But her hands were tied, weren't they? If she tried to defend herself there wouldn't be a wedding. It was as simple as that, and the repercussions of such a cancellation would be on her own head. Why not let Rick Conway believe what he had been told? After the wedding she needn't see him again, so what did it matter what he thought of her? It probably wouldn't make any difference to her reputation. Plenty of girls slept around these days and no one appeared to think anything of it.

'I can look after myself,' she said at last, lowering tormented eyes so he wouldn't see her pain.

'I realise you can, if to begin with you had me fooled,' he returned tightly. 'If Rex hadn't spilled the beans it would have dawned as I danced with you. I knew then you were no prim teenager. The way you moved against me was provocative, to say the least. It had every bone in my body crying for release. If I'd had the chance, there and then you'd have been under me.'

Infuriated, Emma shot her hand out to slap his leering face hard. 'You're—oh, I can't find words bad enough!' she cried helplessly. 'No man's going to speak to me like that. I could be a—a tramp!'

'That's the impression I got,' he grinned contemptuously, as he turned on his heel and left her.

Emma didn't see Rick again before he departed for Australia. For once she was grateful to be left out of the family's social activities. As soon as she heard he was gone she told both her aunt and cousin she had no wish to attend the forthcoming wedding. Hilda, obviously thinking this would mean less expense, replied smoothly that it might be as well, as someone would have to stay and look after the farm. They couldn't all be away.

The calculating swiftness with which Hilda provided her with an excuse might, at any other time, have hurt, but Emma was only aware of relief. She had no wish to see Rick Conway married, to her cousin or anyone else—not after all he had said and done! Not only had he treated her badly, he had spoken to her as she suspected no man spoke to a woman for whom he had any respect.

Every nerve in her body still trembled with resentment each time she remembered. If she had been able to give herself the satisfaction of straightening him out, it might have been worth it, if only to have seen his face. This she had to deny herself, both for Blanche's sake and, Emma was secrectly ashamed to admit, her own. To get rid of Blanche, not to have her constantly around with her spiteful tongue and endless commands, was surely worth a little sacrifice of pride and self-respect. Somehow she managed to ignore the whisper inside her which suggested the cost was too great. What did she care what an arrogant sugar plantation owner thought of her? She'd be the biggest fool on earth if she did.

It was just over a week later that Blanche burst into her bedroom. 'Mother's out,' she said, without preamble, 'I have to talk to you.'

Emma, busy mending a pair of the woollen socks she wore on the farm, glanced up frowning. Blanche's face wore an expression which was not unfamiliar. She was intensely excited about something. Just what was she up to? Usually Emma was left to guess, but she was nervous rather than gratified that, this time, Blanche apparently wanted to confide in her. Something warned her that she wasn't going to like what was coming.

Despite the haste with which Blanche had descended on her cousin, she appeared in no great hurry to unburden herself. She strolled to the window and stared out at the rolling downs which were so much a feature of the South Country. They weren't far from London, but no one could have guesssed as the farm was lonely and isolated.

'You're back early today, aren't you?' When Blanche didn't speak, Emma made an effort to find out what all the agitation was about. She had no desire to be on the receiving end of Blanche's confidences and she wished the other girl had waited until her mother returned.

Blanche swung around, at the sound of Emma's voice, as though her mind was quite made up. 'I'm going to Paris for a few days. With Rex,' she enlarged coldly, defying Emma to query it.

Emma was too bewildered to say anything immediately, but the shocked apprehension in her eyes said it for her. She just blinked at Blanche and swallowed.

'I'm not a child, Emma,' Blanche exclaimed tartly,

reading things in Emma's face she didn't care for. 'I know what I'm doing, so you needn't start asking what about Rick. He doesn't have to know a thing about it.'

'But—why?' Emma whispered, horrified. 'I mean, you're about to be married. And what if Rick does find out? What then?'

'He won't.'

'How can you be so sure?' Emma's voice was stiff with disapproval. 'Besides, it's not fair!'

'Shut up, you sanctimonious little saint!' Blanche was suddenly spitting venom. 'You don't know Rick. Once we're married he'll come down with a heavy hand. His wife will have to toe the line in every way, both in bed and out. He's not really the lazy, sardonic character you might think he is.'

Colouring vividly at Blanche's over-candid remarks, Emma chose to ignore what she considered the worst of them. Neither Rick nor Blanche had any qualms about embarrassing her, but it annoyed her nearly as much that they could so easily make her blush. 'If you feel this way about Rick, why marry him, for heaven's sake?'

'Haven't I told you before?' Blanche chaffed impatiently. 'Freedom from work, all that lovely sunshine and money, but you can believe he'll demand his money's worth!'

'You don't have to force me, I'm quite convinced,' Emma retorted dryly, recalling with a tremor the powerful litheness of Rick Conway's body, the decisive lines etched on his face. 'Yet money isn't everything, Blanche. Neither is a life of leisure, I shouldn't think.'

'I shan't complain,' Blanche sneered.

'I still don't understand how you can even consider marrying him when you love Rex.'

'Are you crazy?' Blanche cried. 'I certainly don't harbour any tender feelings for Rex. I'm attracted to him, that's all, and he's helped me a lot with my career.'

There was a lot here which was beyond her. Emma felt hopelessly inadequate as she gazed at her cousin. How did one even begin to deal with such a problem—if Blanche's imminent betrayal of her fiancé could be classed as such. One thing was quite obvious, Blanche wasn't looking for advice, good or otherwise. All the same, Emma tried to give some. 'Why not forget about Rex and concentrate on Rick's wealth?' Blanche had always been greedy. 'I'm sure he intends giving you a good time, and I don't think he regards you as a business proposition at all. In fact he did say he hasn't looked at another woman since he met you.'

'All of three months ago!' Blanche's mouth, a little on the thin side, curled.

'On an island like Barbados, surely that must prove that he cares for you. There must be plenty of lovely women, enough temptation?'

'I know perfectly well what there is on Barbados,' Blanche snapped, 'but he doesn't stay there all the time. He has other places in the Caribbean. One island in particular is completely isolated and he enjoys staying there for months on end. That's probably where he's been the last three months, avoiding temptation. There, I've been told, he often supervises the work personally, but if he thinks I'm going to bury myself there for weeks on end, he can think again!'

'It must be because he's interested in what he's doing there,' Emma suggested reasonably. 'I can't somehow imagine him doing anything he didn't want to do.'

'Don't ask me,' Blanche retorted sharply. 'It can't have missed your avid little ears that I scarcely know Rick at all. Sometimes I wonder if he'll suit me. I've heard a rumour that he's a very sensuous man.'

'Then if I felt that way, I wouldn't marry him!' Emma made an effort to emulate Blanche's disconcerting frankness. 'I would simply tell him I'd changed my mind.'

'You wouldn't say that if you had a chance of marrying him,' Blanche mocked.

'You seem determined to throw yours away.'

'No, I don't,' Blanche replied smugly. 'I certainly intend being Mrs Rick Conway, but I also intend having a last fling, first, even if it kills me.'

'Supposing Rick does?'

'He won't find out, not if you promise to help me.'

'Me?' Wild fright tore through Emma's young breast as she visualised being on the receiving end of Rick's anger. Already she'd had one sample of his quick fury, she didn't want another!

Blanche ignored her protests as she had been doing for years. Emma couldn't expect her not to. 'All I'm asking you to do,' she said coldly, 'is to tell Rick, if he rings, that I'm visiting my aunt Helen, who we all know doesn't have the phone in. I'm taking Mother there tomorrow to stay with her for a few days as she hasn't been well and can't come to the wedding. So if Rick were to check in that direction, and I don't imagine for a moment he will, it wouldn't occur to him to check which of us was actually staying with Aunt Helen.'

Amazed at Blanche's barefaced duplicity, Emma exclaimed, 'What if Rick asks your mother about it, when he gets back?'

'Don't worry—he won't. Why should he?' Blanche, supremely confident, shrugged her shoulders. 'To make sure, I'll have a word with Mother later. She won't let me down.'

'And you're asking me to help deceive Rick, too?'

'Oh, come off it!' Blanche sneered with exasperation. 'Is there any need to be so dramatic? Why not pretend you have no wish to see him hurt, if it's your conscience that's worrying you? I'm sure if you look at it that way it won't be too difficult. You were always a charitable little thing.'

'I—I still don't know . . .'

'Well, tell him the truth—any damn thing you like!' Blanche flung out of the bedroom in a fury. 'Tell him what suits you. I don't care. But I'm going to Paris with Rex!'

As the door slammed behind her, Emma blinked at it in an agony of dismay, realising it would be impossible to tell Rick that kind of truth. She knew it and so did Blanche. If Blanche failed to get her own way by what she considered logical argument, she resorted to a craftiness which seldom failed.

The house was quiet with no one to occupy it but herself, and Emma's nerves grew jagged as she daily anticipated Rick ringing from Australia. He had been in touch once, just before Blanche went away, and it was unlikely, Blanche said, that he would ring again until the end of the week, but one never knew.

Blanche had, before she had left for Paris, broken the uneasy silence which had existed between the two girls ever since the scene in Emma's bedroom. She had reluctantly told Emma the name of the luxury hotel where she would be staying with Rex. She had parted with this information only because she and her mother had found Helen much worse than they had expected, and her doctor had warned she might not have long to live.

'Don't contact me unless the old girl pops off,' Blanche had instructed callously, while threatening dire repercussions should Emma dare divulge her whereabouts to anyone else.

Emma, hearing Rex tooting loudly at the door, as if running off with another man's fiancée wasn't something to keep quiet about, had been inclined to go and confront him. He and Blanche might be a well matched pair, but at least Rex wasn't engaged to someone else. Somewhere under all that worldly, sophisticated boredom might lie one spark of decency.

'Don't you dare!' Blanche had hissed, as Emma hesitated, clearly guessing her intentions.

'It might be worth a try.' Emma had stared at her cousin bravely.

'What if you succeeded?' Blanche had mocked. 'Would you offer to take my place? Somehow I think you'd find Paris a bit too much for you.'

Ignoring the other girl's scorn, Emma frowned. Hadn't Blanche known she had been there several times? Emma's father had sometimes taken her to Paris during school holidays to stay with a relation of her mother's. Once they had spent Christmas there. Her mother's cousin had owned a rather grand house—she probably still did. Ruefully, Emma glanced down at her work-worn hands, wondering wryly what the so elegant Clarice would make of them. She remembered her as distinctly *grande dame* and very beautiful. There had been a time when Emma feared her father might be thinking of marrying her, and, though nothing had come of it, they had never gone back after Clarice had married another man.

While she had stood there pondering over the past and hesitating, Blanche had picked up her smart suitcase and gone, leaving Emma to realise unhappily that she had lost the only chance she was likely to get of making either Blanche or Rex change their minds.

CHAPTER THREE

RICK CONWAY didn't ring, after all. He arrived in person the morning after Blanche left, ten days before he was due back.

The shock was almost too much for Emma. He didn't bother to knock, which might, she thought, have given her intuition time to warn her. It seemed grossly unfair that the first intimation she had of his presence was when he opened the kitchen door and walked in.

In view of the terrible seriousness of the situation, Emma had great difficulty in restraining a hysterical laugh when he asked casually, 'How is it, if you're in the house, you're always to be found in the kitchen?'

She was too stunned to answer that. She had just been out in the fields with coffee for Jim and had been about to have her own before starting on the account books. 'You aren't supposed to be here!' she whispered.

'Well, I can't think of anywhere else I'd rather be at the moment,' he drawled. 'Where's Blanche?'

'Bl—Blanche?' In his rather expressionless face she sensed tension, but it couldn't be as great as her own.

Suddenly his eyes narrowed alarmingly as he threw off his coat. 'If she's out tell me where. And I don't want any more stories about not knowing!'

Oh, God, how did she get out of this one? Behind Rick's tension was determination. It stood out a mile. Joining it, as she stood gaping at him like a landed fish, was suspicion, which warned her she must act quickly if she was to avert worse. 'I—I think she's gone abroad, but don't ask me where.'

'Exactly what you said last time,' he rejoined grimly, 'only this time you've decided to have her abroad.'

41

'How would I know exactly where she's gone?' Emma gasped, her grey eyes flashing, knowing suddenly that aggression might be her only defence. 'It's none of my business and I don't ask. You'd better try London, her agency or somewhere. I'm busy—so if you'll excuse me?'

She would never have believed that in grasping her and whipping her off her feet, Rick could have acted so swiftly. One moment she was standing, defying him, the next he had caught her up, like a hurricane. In an instant she was over his knee, his hand descending without mercy on the seat of her pants, while she screamed with temper and pain.

'Let me go, you great brute, or I'll call the police!'

He was deaf. The hand continued to rise and fall with renewed vigour. 'I'll stop when you agree to talk,' he snapped harshly, ignoring her wild threats.

He meant it as well! Emma groaned aloud, choking. Hadn't Blanche told her he spent a lot of time in isolated, uncivilised places? She had been right about the veneer, too. Rick Conway's easygoing drawl was only skin-deep. The cruel savagery underneath it was being transmitted only too clearly through the force of his hand.

Tears were running down Emma's cheeks before she gave in. 'Please stop!' she begged, the hardness of his thighs pressing against her small breasts arousing a sensation almost as hard to bear as the pain he was inflicting on her delicately rounded posterior.

'Had enough?' he enquired laconically.

She nodded, blindly, in abject humiliation. 'I hate you!' she cried, as he released her.

'That's neither here nor there.'

As she stood up she felt dizzy and hurt all over. 'You can go to . . . No!' she shrieked, as his hand shot out to grab her again.

Pausing, he snapped, 'Then spill the beans. I'm not interested in where you'd like to see me.'

Emma was. She could have killed him! The horrible dizziness persisted, so she scarcely knew what she was saying. It took away any strength she had left to fight him.

'Where is she, Emma?'

'She's in Paris,' Emma hiccupped, feeling it had been torn out of her, but that was all she was going to say. She lifted huge, tear-drenched eyes to meet his, daring him to ask more.

'With?'

'With . . .?' Emma tried her best to look blank.

'Out with it!' The hard bones of his jaw and chin tightened. 'I want answers, Emma, not evasion—or else!'

The implications of that couldn't have been clearer. As it was she might not be able to sit down for days. More tears ran, she couldn't seem to stop them, but there was no pity in Rick's hard, unrelenting face. All the same, she did try to make one last effort on behalf of the girl who had always treated her as something less than human. 'I won't,' she gasped, 'I can't tell you!'

'Yes, you can.' He grasped her hair, this time, having some difficulty in getting his hands through the thickness of it, but succeeding painfully.

'Oh . . .' she moaned, hating him so much yet unable to retaliate. There was one way she could be revenged, but she was reluctant to take it. It took a second cruel tug on her hair to make her decide furiously that Rick deserved to be hurt, as much as he was hurting her. Fury and fright, momentarily eliminating discretion, she sobbed, 'She's with Rex!'

'Ah . . .' it was a long-drawn-out sigh of cold anger. For a second he stood so still Emma shuddered. 'So I was right to cut short my visit down under. The little bitch! I'd like to . . .'

Emma tried to close her ears to what he said next, but even if she had managed to do so completely it would have been obvious from his expression that Blanche had burnt her boats in every direction, so far as he was concerned. Anxiously she sought for something to say that might make him feel better, but could anything soothe a man in such circumstances?

'Blanche didn't mean you to know anything about it,' was the best she could manage. 'I'm sure she didn't mean to hurt you.'

'Is that supposed to help?' he snarled.

Emma spread her hands, her face pale. 'What more can I say?'

'I expect you knew what was going on?' he attacked her again, his voice harsh and grating. 'You must have known you were fighting a losing battle over Rex Oliver. You knew what might easily happen, yet you never thought to warn me.'

'Would you have listened?' she whispered, aghast at his twisted interpretation of things.

'If you hadn't been so busy trying to hang on to Oliver by the skin of your teeth, you might have had time to think of other people!'

'You don't exactly inspire anyone to worry over you, Rick,' she couldn't resist pointing out. 'You always seem capable of handling everything.'

'Are you being sarcastic?' he gazed at her, his eyes like steel. 'I can handle most things, but not something I know nothing about. Then I have to rely on instinct, which is what brought me back ten days before I was due.'

'If only I'd been able to speak to Rex!' Emma felt with anguished certainty that she should have made a greater effort.

'Would he have listened?' Rick Conway ran a contemptuous eye over her unprepossessing figure. 'It's quite clear to me now he was only using you for one thing, and I doubt if he derived much pleasure even from that.'

As Emma gasped in rage and horror, he continued, his

anger apparently no less than her own, 'You could have come off worse. He could have persuaded you to go to Paris with him instead of Blanche. But before you begin congratulating yourself, don't think you're going to get away with it. You have a lot to answer for, bringing a man like that to the house, conspiring to fool me!'

'I——' Emma began, then paused. What was the use of trying to convince him she wasn't guilty? He would never believe her, and in another few minutes he could be gone. Yet suddenly, for all she hated him intensely for what he had just done to her, she knew an urgent desire to prove she was innocent, at least of most of the things he was accusing her of. After all, neither Blanche or Rex could have anything more to lose. She had to make sure, though.

'Couldn't you possibly forgive Blanche?' she whispered. 'Don't you still love her? Surely no one can stop loving, just like that?'

'Love?' he sneered mockingly, but when Emma waited to hear more, he changed the subject. 'I'm not good at forgiving people, least of all girls who go off with other men. I certainly don't intend forgiving Blanche, nor do I intend letting her go scot-free. Like you, she'll pay for her sins.'

'I hope you're not contemplating anything foolish,' Emma gulped miserably. 'It's so easy to do something we regret afterwards.'

'You'll be with me all the way,' he promised, his eyes glinting coldly, 'so you'll see whether I have any regrets or not.'

What was he talking about? Not caring for the almost sinister ring in his voice, Emma wasn't sure she really wanted to know. She was tired and wished he would go quickly and leave her in peace. There'd be more re-criminations when Blanche came home and she didn't know how much more she could take. As she gazed in weary perplexity at Rick Conway all her former desire to vindicate herself in his eyes left her. If she had any desire now it was simply to see the last of him.

'I'm afraid,' she said numbly, 'I don't quite follow you, but I think it would be better if you went. I don't feel so good myself. In some ways I think I've suffered almost as great a shock as you have.'

'We have to talk,' he stared back at her coldly, without even the smallest flicker of sympathy in his eyes.

'All the talk in the world isn't going to make any difference,' she rejoined stubbornly. 'Before you say any more I feel you should see Blanche. There could be a very simple explanation.'

'Sex and a good time, with someone else's property,' he replied scathingly. 'On second thoughts, sex probably doesn't really come into it. She was always a cold little b . . .'

'Don't dare say it!' Her cheeks burning, Emma cut in. 'I don't have to listen to that kind of talk. I refuse to speak to you again!'

'You're going to do more than that,' his mouth twisting savagely, he delivered a bombshell, 'you're going to marry me.'

'Just like that?' she gasped, unable to believe he wasn't joking.

'Yes, just like that,' he assured her, a hard glint in his eyes. 'I've always made decisions quickly and my intuition rarely lets me down. I could say never, but not after Blanche. Blanche, I'll admit, didn't work out, but you will, if I have to drag you to the altar. We'll be married and spend our honeymoon in Paris. At the same hotel as your cousin and your late boy-friend.'

Emma thought she might choke with stunned surprise. She still couldn't believe he was serious. Yet he had such a look of grim determination that in spite of herself she was half convinced. 'You must be crazy,' she whispered hoarsely, 'even to be contemplating such a thing!'

'I mean it, Emma,' he rasped, standing over her, very tall and formidable, giving more than a hint of what she would have to fight if she didn't immediately obey him. 'I have a marriage licence—your name fortunately is Davis, too, and I believe Blanche's second name is also Emma, after your paternal grandmother, so there shouldn't be any difficulty there.'

Staring at him, her grey eyes widening, Emma was suddenly afraid. 'The whole idea is ridiculous,' she faltered. 'Why don't you try being sensible for a change? How do you know Blanche didn't change her mind? She might still be in London, nowhere near Paris.'

'I can certainly check.' His voice vibrated with a derision which, spreading to his eyes, scorched her. 'Lead me to your telephone.'

Emma, wondering anxiously what he was going to say, showed him into the small study where the books she had been about to begin work on were piled on the desk. When she turned to leave his hand shot out to catch her wrist. 'Stay with me,' he commanded. 'I don't want you to disappear.'

What he meant, she supposed, was that he didn't want her disappearing into the countryside, leaving him to carry out his devious plans alone. On the way from the kitchen he had asked the name of the hotel where Blanche and Rex were staying, and while she had momentarily toyed with the notion of pretending she didn't know, a glint in Rick's eye had warned her it would be a waste of time.

Cynically, he had shrugged. 'It's one of the best. I haven't stayed there personally, but I know of people who have. Meanness can't be another of Oliver's vices.'

Waiting, while Rick put through his call, Emma felt a mass of nerves. A de luxe hotel in most capital cities would have an international switchboard, but she wasn't really

surprised when he used fluent French. If the state of her
nerves hadn't been good when he started, they were worse
by the time he had finished. Blanche was there, she
gathered, listening apprehensively as Rick Conway cun-
ningly extracted the information. She had been there since
last night. Emma's heart felt like lead, but before Rick
put down the receiver something else was disturbing her
even more.

'She is there,' he snapped, turning to her, his face taut
with anger, 'staying quite openly as Mrs Rex Oliver.'

'Are you sure?'

'Sure!' he laughed curtly. 'I got an adequate description
and I'm more than satisfied. Blanche was fond of saying
that no one ever looks for the obvious, and your friend
Oliver must believe he has nothing to lose.'

While trying to assimilate this, Emma heard herself
murmuring in painful apprehension, 'Is it true you've
booked rooms from tomorrow?'

Sharply he glanced at her shaken face. 'You could
follow what I was saying?'

'A little.' She didn't bother explaining, although she
sensed his surprise, 'Are you—' she swallowed and had to
make another attempt, 'Are you going after them?'

'Not with a gun in my hand.' His black brows rose
above eyes hard as steel. 'A wife will be a much better
weapon, as I've already told you.'

'No!' Emma cried.

He took no notice of her protesting anguish, but continued ruthlessly as if she had never spoken.

'We'll leave for London this morning, after I settle
things here. Tomorrow we get married, then pop over the
Channel. You might even enjoy the experience.'

'You're mad!' she repeated unevenly. 'Quite mad!' Her
eyes darkened to twin pools of fear. 'I—I don't see how
you can enjoy such a joke, after what's just happened!'

'It's because of what's happened, you little fool,' he

snarled, while his grasp on her thin shoulders threatened to break her in two. 'Listen to me,' he said grimly, his dark eyes boring into hers. 'We both want revenge, but if that was all that mattered I have no doubt it could easily be achieved without marriage. Certainly I have no great wish to be tied to a pitiful little nobody like you, but I have no wish, either, to return to my home minus the bride whom a great many of my friends and relations are waiting to see. I refuse to become an object of ridicule.'

Smarting under his contemptuous remarks, Emma retorted tersely, 'What's to stop you saying you'd been the one to change your mind?'

'Lies of that kind are almost always found out,' he replied.

Desperately she suggested next. 'You must know a lot of beautiful women who'd be only too willing to marry you—for any reason whatsoever.'

'Several,' he agreed, without batting an arrogant eyelid, 'but if I were to marry one of them Blanche would eventually get over the fact that through her own foolishness she lost herself a millionaire. You, my dear Emma, as her cousin, will prove a constant reminder. Plain women can be draped in furs and jewels, all the outward trappings of success, just as easily as beautiful ones. And even though she might seldom see you she won't find it possible to forget.'

'Aren't you rather cutting off your nose to spite your face?' Emma argued helplessly. 'Don't forget you'll have to live with me, not Blanche. Rather than grinding her teeth in anger, she might just as easily finish up pitying you for being tied to an unattractive wife.'

'Don't worry,' he snapped, 'it won't be for long. Just as long as it takes to really hurt.'

And who would suffer most, Emma wondered dismally, in the meantime? Worry gnawed holes in her stomach as she viewed with apprehension the lengths to which a man

might be prepared to go to avenge his wounded pride. Of
course Rick Conway loved Blanche and that must be
hurting too, but she doubted if love was the most important emotion behind the force that seemed to be driving
him.

'Aren't you forgetting something?' She stared up at him
mutinously. 'For all you despise me, you need me to
help carry out your awful plans, and I refuse!'

'No, you won't,' he said roughly. 'Not unless you're
more of a fool than I take you to be. You'll be able to
laugh at your ex-lover and get away from here. Not only
that, you'll be able to lead a life of luxurious idleness for
at least a year—and without the embarrassment of a husband invading your bedroom, demanding his rights. The
lack of sex, of course, is the one thing that might really
worry you, but I'm sure there'll be compensations. You'll
find it a small price to pay for what I'm prepared to give
you otherwise.'

'You're insulting!' Emma cried, every inch of her body
burning beneath his acrimonious tongue.

'I can afford to be,' he assured her indifferently. 'Why
not try thinking of Oliver's face when he hears you've
captured an even bigger fish than he is? It might help.'

'I still won't . . .'

Rick cut her off coldly, his dark face aloof, as though
he had had more than enough of what he clearly considered her senseless protesting. 'I have a couple of calls
to make. While I'm busy, why not go and fix us some
coffee and think things over? I'm sure you'll come round
to seeing things my way in a very short time.'

He might have been planning a business deal.
Completely incredulous, Emma turned without another
word and went into the kitchen. After starting the coffee
she slumped down at the table. That, of course, was
exactly what he was planning, a business deal, but did he
realise completely what he was doing? He was bound to

be suffering from some degree of shock, and shock could make people react in the most peculiar ways. He must have loved Blanche a lot.

An odd ache began in Emma's heart when she considered that, but she wasn't sure if it was for herself or Rick? Blanche deserved to suffer—Rick was right in this respect. What he didn't seem to understand was that revenge had a funny way of rebounding on those who carried it out. She had a very uneasy feeling that, in the end, she might be the one to suffer most if she agreed to marry Rick and went to Paris with him.

If that had been all it might have been bad enough, but afterwards there would be his family to face. Blanche had never talked of Rick's family, so Emma knew nothing about them, but she did know that families could be very intuitive about each other. What was to stop Rick's relatives from finding out about his bogus marriage and making her a target for their subsequent scorn and amusement?

And what, she forced herself to ask, with an odd little quiver, if the awareness she already felt for him turned into something deeper? She might hate him, but this peculiar emotion she felt seemed stronger than hate or anything else. When he had grasped her shoulders a few minutes ago he had hurt, but she had also felt a sensation running through her, akin to the blaze of a newly lighted fire.

While some vague, shivering premonition of danger warned her to run while she still had the chance, it was fear of another kind that finally decided Emma to do as Rick asked. When Blanche returned and discovered what had happened she would be furious, to say the least. And if Emma stayed she had no doubt the other girl would make her life intolerable. Then, if she had to leave the farm without money, a career or a home, where would she go? What would happen to her? What hope would she have of ever finding another job? Whereas, if she was to marry Rick, hadn't he more or less promised he would see her well provided for? He might divorce her, but he wouldn't see her destitute. Marriage would at least give her time to look around and to make plans for the future.

Her mind made up uneasily at last, Emma still remained uncertain about several things, one of which she considered important. She was convinced Rick mustn't know Rex Oliver had never been her lover. If Rick was to suspect she was marrying him just to escape being here when Blanche returned, then he might change his mind. And suddenly Emma's fear of Blanche was strangely greater than her fear of him. If he were to learn that she was innocent of all he accused her of, he would probably tell her to forget the whole thing. Then where would she be? Surely a marriage in name only, for one short year, would be a small price to pay for a fresh start?

Having reached a decision, Emma stuck to it resolutely, and to her surprise was able to face Rick a few minutes later with remarkable composure.

It caused her some chagrin, after all her painful soul-searching, that he appeared to have taken her capitulation for granted. He accepted her willingness to marry him as casually as he drank the two cups of black coffee she made him.

'Go upstairs and pack your things,' he said, his face expressionless. 'We leave at once.'

'At once?' she gasped, almost spilling her own coffee, which she suddenly didn't want. 'I—I can't leave right away, Rick. I'll have to speak to Jim first. Then there's the house.'

'I'll go and see Jim while you're packing,' he said curtly. 'Go on.'

Still she hesitated. 'I'm not sure that Jim can manage on his own.' Anxiously she met Rick's eyes, 'It's crazy to think I can just walk out!'

'Jim will—and you can,' Rick replied tightly. 'We had quite a chat, Jim and I, over your cow and calf last week. You have very little livestock and your spring crops are all in. It won't be beyond him to manage until your aunt returns to make other arrangements.'

'If you say so,' Emma whispered, wondering why she was giving in so weakly, when her conscience was protesting so strongly. His mention of Hilda and Blanche couldn't have anything to do with it.

Rushing upstairs as though the devil himself was after her, she was trying to find something suitable for London when she glanced up to find Rick leaning against the bedroom door, watching her. He hadn't been long, and she almost jumped with fright.

'Get out!' she exclaimed, reacting to his presence with instinctive alarm. 'We aren't married yet.'

Coolly his eyes mocked her flushed cheeks. 'Don't flatter yourself that I came for anything—or ever will, not from you.'

Her lips trembled against his unexpected hardness. 'I'm sorry,' she mumbled, her face hotter than ever, 'I didn't mean ... I mean, I won't expect ...'

'I'm glad you understand,' he stared at her insolently. 'I thought I'd made that very clear, but perhaps I'd better refresh your memory. It is only in public that I'll ask you to endure being near me—for appearances' sake.'

'While, in private, you ignore me?' she choked, unable to understand why she should feel so bleak about it.

'Oh, I might not ignore you altogether,' he rejoined derisively. 'I don't imagine I could love you, but I do believe I might enjoy schooling you. A little tough handling might be good for you at that. It might help straighten you out while you're still young enough to be reformed. Like your cousin, you've obviously inherited a twisted character from somewhere.'

Apprehensively Emma's thoughts leaped to her father.

Rick must never find out that his business had failed when he'd tried to take a short cut by cheating somebody. At least so Hilda had said. When, with what must have been coincidence, Rick asked sharply what her father's employment had been, she muttered something about him being out of work when he'd died.

As if the paleness of her face warned him against probing further, Rick straightened abruptly from the door. 'I don't want to hear any more. Just close your case and I'll take it to the car while you dress.'

'I'm afraid I haven't much,' she indicated uncertainly to the few shabby articles of clothing the case contained, which was all she had. 'I've two photographs, though, of my parents,' she showed him the parcel, neatly wrapped in newspaper, tied with string. 'Please,' her eyes were huge and anxious, 'I have to keep them.'

'I'm not a monster,' he assured her impatiently. 'Take what you like.' Removing them from her tightly protective clasp, he almost flung them on top of her clothes, snapping the case shut himself. 'Now get a move on,' he commanded curtly, viewing her trembling figure grimly. 'I won't tell you again. If you aren't down in five minutes I'll leave without you.'

Emma never could decide whether he had really been giving her a chance to change her mind or not. She dressed swiftly, obeying him weakly. It made her contemptuous of herself, all the way to London, that she hadn't been able to find the courage to defy him and stay.

Once in the city, she was amazed at how quickly Rick got things done. He was so decisive and competent she didn't think she would ever be able to keep up with him. After arranging for them to stay at a luxurious and discreetly quiet hotel, he took her to a fashionable boutique and bought her some new clothes.

When she hissed a protest when the saleswoman's back

was turned, he merely looked bored. 'You need something for dinner tonight, and to get married in. What you're wearing at the moment wouldn't flatter a tramp.'

'Oh, I hate you!' she cried.

'It's no use trying to look like a wounded gazelle,' he jeered. 'I suppose you're so shabby because you couldn't bear to bring the things you wore when you went out with Oliver?'

Startled, she glanced at him, nervously moving her head. This, she realised too late, he took for acquiescence. But, as she sought belatedly to correct the assumption, it occurred to her that she couldn't. Not if she wanted her secret to remain safe. If Rick knew she had no other clothes he would immediately become suspicious—and, because of his astuteness, that need only be a short step to his guessing the true state of affairs between herself and Rex Oliver.

Without another murmur she chose two outfits, and when she tried them on she fancied Rick was surprised at her good taste. The small hairdressing salon which Rick found next enhanced her image a little more. Her hair, when she emerged, looked a lot better than it had done when she went in, and she purchased some moisture cream for her neglected skin. Perhaps in Paris or Barbados she might have time to consult someone who could advise her properly about it. Working out on the farm in all weathers hadn't seemed to improve its appearance.

She passed her wedding day in a kind of vague daze, finding nothing in the brief ceremony to convince her she was really getting married. From the time she rose in the morning to the moment when she and Rick entered the impressive foyer of the hotel on the Rue de Rivoli in Paris, she felt she couldn't be certain she wasn't dreaming. Curiously, if she was nervous it wasn't of Rick. He had been a remote stranger since they left the farm. In everything he had done, from the buying of her dresses to her engagement and wedding rings, he had kept his distance. As she stood beside him, repeating the vows which changed her status, in an incredibly few minutes, from Miss Emma Davis to Mrs Richard Conway, he had seemed more distant than ever. Her hand had trembled when he lifted it to slip the gold wedding ring on her long, slender finger. She feared her lips had trembled, too, when his mouth had touched them swiftly in a brief, formal kiss. Apart from this she had had no great difficulty in controlling her feelings. She was even beginning to believe in her own impassivity until the doors of their splendidly furnished suite closed behind them and she and Rick were alone.

Trying to pretend an interest in the beautiful room, rather than stare at her tall, handsome bridegroom, Emma started to hear him say, 'I've ordered dinner up here. I don't think we'll confront Blanche and Rex until tomorrow.'

Emma gasped, turning to him quickly, her eyes widening at the smoothness of his tones. 'You—you don't intend knocking Rex down, do you? Hurting him?'

Harshly he laughed at her obvious anxiety. 'No, my dear child, I won't go as far as that. You need have no great fear for your lover.'

Unhappily Emma lowered her head, wishing she could tell him the truth, now they were married. Of course she couldn't, since it might only make things worse for Blanche than they were already. Emma was still confused by a mixed-up desire to protect her cousin. Then weren't there her own personal reasons for marrying Rick? She was using him as a means of escape, she reminded herself, which wasn't very admirable either.

Weakly, as a means of distraction, she pounced on something else. 'I wish you wouldn't refer to me as a child, Rick.'

'Nineteen!' Too late she realised his willingness to

return to a subject which had drawn several muttered curses earlier. 'God!' his hands gripped her slender shoulders painfully, his breath cold on her face, 'If we hadn't been in a register office, I think I would have cancelled the whole thing. Nineteen to my thirty-five!' Hardening, his eyes glittered down on her. 'Why didn't you tell me?'

'You said someone had.'

His hands tightened in angry frustration. Bleakly he studied her hot face, as though seeing the very young lines of it for the first time. 'Either Blanche or Rex hinted that you were well over twenty.'

'Well, does it matter?' Emma asked dully. 'Ours isn't meant to be a real marriage, after all.'

A frown cut deeply across his broad forehead, compressing his sensuous mouth. 'Other people will believe it is.'

'You still aren't old enough to be my father,' she smiled faintly. 'Plenty of girls are married at my age, and to slightly older men.'

'Perhaps,' he shrugged, without committing himself. 'In our case it won't be for long.'

Releasing her abruptly, he thrust his hands in his pockets and turned away. Emma turned away, too, as she noticed the tautness of his strong thighs under the tightening cloth. Her breath caught, making her stumble as she fled to the window and stared blindly out. Her heart steadied a little as she watched a light breeze dancing through the tender green leaves and rioting blossom of springtime France. Above them the sky was darkening as night approached, to a beautiful violet blue. A scene for lovers, she thought, feeling suddenly bleak.

'You'd better come and choose your bedroom.' Rick spoke so closely behind her she was startled, but she obeyed as blindly as she had left him. The suite was magnificent, with its bedrooms and bathrooms and spacious lounge. There was more space here than might be found in

many homes, but hadn't Rick said something about being
a millionaire?

She considered the two bedrooms, as he was obviously
waiting for her to make her choice. 'I'll have this one.'
She took the smaller. 'It will do fine.'

He didn't argue or comment on her rather trite remark
as he turned and walked into the other one and closed the
door. Emma blinked at the closed door uncertainly.
Wasn't it the bride who was supposed to do that? With a
funny little sigh she wandered into her own quarters,
dropping her bandbag indifferently on the bed.

Nervously she approached the dressing table, staring at
herself in the glass. The pale, silky two-piece she wore
looked nice. It had been cool for late April in London
and she had felt chilled, but this had been quite in keeping
with her mood as she had married Rick. It hadn't been
until after the ceremony, when he had bent with brief
mockery to kiss her mouth, that she had again been
consumed by the strange sensation of fire which twice
before had overheated her skin. Later she had flinched
from the cynicism in his eyes as she had opened her own
to find him watching her.

'You might have to do better than that,' he had commented, his eyes narrowed, his voice low and taunting.

Anxiously now she wondered what he had meant. She
was sure, at that moment, he hadn't been thinking of
Blanche.

CHAPTER FOUR

SUDDENLY, as confused thoughts tumbled around in Emma's mind, the communicating door between their two rooms opened and Rick came in. He had discarded his jacket, but still wore his shirt and trousers although his shirt was unbuttoned at the neck.

Stealing a glance at his face through the thick veil of her lashes, she tried to keep her leaping senses under control, not foolish enough to imagine he was here seeking his marital rights. He had been frank enough on that subject yesterday. Yet her heart beat uneasily as her lashes swept down on her cheeks. No man surely had the right to look so disturbingly attractive.

'I'm busy settling in,' she said carefully, 'as you can see.'

Glancing about him swiftly, he replied dryly, 'I can't see any great signs of it, but I'll take your word for it. I hoped you might be in your bath.'

'Why?'

'Don't sound so defensive, I had no intention of joining you,' he snapped, disregarding her hot cheeks. 'I thought it might ease some of the tension out of you. You won't see Oliver tonight, you know, so you can forget about that.'

Her eyes widened. 'I wasn't even thinking—and if that's why you're here . . .'

'Not altogether, I'm afraid,' he cut through her muddled sentences sardonically, 'but there's nothing to get alarmed about.'

'Then what . . .?' she stammered nervously, not caring to be teased in this manner. He was beginning to disturb her so easily. Every time he glanced at her she could feel her nerves tauten. Suddenly she wished she were a million miles away.

When, as he drew nearer, her unconscious fears urged her to flee, Rick seemed to anticipate the step she was about to take and his hand shot impatiently out to keep her where she was.

'Don't do that,' he exclaimed irritably. 'That's the reason I'm here. It suddenly occurred to me that you stiffen up like a statue every time I come near you. It won't do at all,' he rasped. 'Our two friends are nothing if not astute. The way you are now they'd guess immediately that you love me no more than I love you.'

Emma's heart went cold at such cruelty, yet what more could she expect? He had married her in anger, and this was no ordinary honeymoon. 'I doubt if they would believe we were in love, no matter how hard we tried to convince them.'

Furiously he retorted, 'But we could pretend it was a case of mutual attraction, if only you'd soften up.'

'It wasn't in the agreement,' she protested.

'It certainly was,' he corrected harshly.

Fearing he was right, she hung her head, feeling, perversely, more rigid than ever. 'You'll have to give me time.'

'That's one thing I can't give you,' he said curtly. 'And unfortunately I can think of only one way to achieve quick results—almost infallible, I've found,' he added contemptuously, 'with stubborn females.'

Before she could move his arms were around her, jerking her to him. As her breath caught in her throat she gave a little cry of sheer fright, and he said roughly against her mouth, 'Can't you damned well relax? Think of it as part of the job. Few people begin a new one without at least some tuition.'

To begin with his mouth crushed hers without gentleness, then, as if trying to keep in mind his own advice, he eased the pressure considerably, even allowing her to breathe. When a slight moan escaped her his hand began softly to caress her narrow back before moving to her nape, to soothe the tension from her neck and shoulders.

'Is that better?' he asked, with what she suspected was a deliberate note of tenderness.

How could she feel better, Emma thought wildly, when she was crushed against him so closely she seemed conscious of every bone in his body? The muscular hardness of his chest was actually hurting her. The dark glitter in his eyes, as she stared dazedly up at him, was too frightening to allow her to relax. It was as if he was momentarily tempted to go farther than this. He was toying with the notion of carrying her to the bed and stripping her naked, of teaching her a lesson she would never forget. She could see he might be considering such a move as a means of revenging himself on Blanche's treachery. Any woman might do.

'Please don't,' she whispered, terrified, yet feeling her heart skipping a beat as his sensuous lips came nearer.

As though he had decided gentleness was getting him nowhere, his mouth hardened as it descended on hers. This time he forced her bruised lips apart and began a ruthless exploration, while his hand curved the back of her head, holding her immobile. It struck her, as she was made to endure a lesson he seemed bent on teaching, that he was a man who didn't really know the meaning of tenderness. Long ago as a child he might have done, but not now. Anything he had learnt in his childhood was now forgotten.

Strangely enough, much as she tried to resist, Emma's frozen body began to change beneath the expert persuasiveness of his lovemaking. Flames began blazing deep down inside her, melting the ice. The beat of her heart accelerated as his arms tightened passionately.

'You're improving,' he muttered thickly, his hands moving to her breasts.

She was vaguely aware of his body hardening and he wasn't bothering to hide the rising desire in his eyes either. There was also surprise, she fancied, that he could feel it for her. This Emma found as humiliating as a shower of cold water. Suddenly, with an anguished little gasp, she wrenched herself from his arms.

Her swift movement darkened his face and she knew a fleeting apprehension until he decided to let her go. Her own reactions surprised her, as a peculiar urgency to rush back into his arms proved almost too strong to resist. She was glad she had, however, when cold indifference swiftly replaced the smouldering passion which had lain in his eyes only moments earlier.

Unable to look at him, Emma stared down at the floor, ashamed that she had responded to him even briefly. Innocent though she was, she recognised that Rick was unused to the slightest rebuff, that usually he only needed to use a little of the experience he had gained over the years in order to get his own way. Obviously, with other women, the slightest assertion of his undeniable masculinity was all he had ever found necessary to have them practically begging at his feet. If he had failed with Blanche, Emma suddenly suspected, it was because he had never really tried.

'Are you feeling any better?' she heard him asking savagely, his almost threatening tone forcing her to raise her head.

'No, I'm not!' she retorted angrily, realising too late she would have been wiser to have pretended she did.

'Then perhaps we should keep on trying?' his silky voice confirmed her fears. 'Perhaps if we both got rid of a few clothes the situation might improve?'

She would have hit him then if he hadn't seen it coming and swiftly caught her flying hand. It could be as well, in future, to remember how quickly he reacted. Again she felt deprived of most of her breath. Her cheeks flaming, it took her all her time to speak. 'I married you and we did have an agreement of sorts. But it didn't include taking my clothes off!'

'What difference is that going to make?' he snapped. 'We can't get the marriage annulled, as we might have done, had you been an innocent little virgin. With your history, all the money in the world wouldn't convince anybody of that.'

Almost as angry as he was, she spluttered, 'You won't talk to me like that again!'

'I wasn't thinking of more talk,' he replied, with brutal frankness. 'It was bed I had in mind.'

She didn't like the way his cold eyes glittered over her, lingering on her thin face and body as if trying to discover, in spite of himself, what was holding him intrigued. Hating the way her limbs were beginning to tremble, she retorted with fury, 'You wouldn't want to go to—to bed with a plain girl like me.'

'Plain or pretty,' he ran derisive fingers over her taut lips, 'what does it matter in the dark?'

'It matters to me.' Emma swallowed convulsively, suddenly unable to bear his mockery—or having him touch her. 'I refuse to go to bed with a man I hate!'

As if to punish her he seemed about to drag her swiftly to him but suddenly he was pushing her away. 'You've a lot to learn,' he said cynically. 'Sometimes hating or loving doesn't come into it. A lot of things are possible without either. Oliver obviously didn't get far with your education.'

As she stared at him, full of dazed uncertainty, he added harshly, 'Don't forget, if Blanche comes here, you have a part to play. And heaven help you if you let me down.'

'Please, Rick!' Emma, her nerve deserting her, was nearly in tears. 'Why not call the whole thing off? I'll go back to England and you can return to your own home. This all seems so silly . . .'

'No,' his mouth tightened as he shook his head, his eyes smouldering darkly, 'I may have some regrets myself. It's not something I would do again, but we'll see it through, since we've got this far.'

In the face of such ruthless determination, Emma could think of nothing more to say, and while she searched helplessly for something else to deter him, Rick turned abruptly and left her. As he quietly closed the door behind him she stared at it, not really seeing it as his strongly modelled face swam before her eyes.

Why was he being so insistent? Were all men like that? Rick, she felt instinctively, would receive few insults, and the few he did would be mostly ignored. Blanche, obviously, must have dealt a blow to his pride and the devil in him was demanding retribution. This Rick would probably be the first to admit, cynically, while refusing to ignore, for once, a desire for revenge. Perhaps if he had given himself time to think at the farm he would have acted differently. But then everything had happened so quickly that common sense had had little chance to intervene. Or had he been too busy planning to ride roughshod over other people's feelings to take any notice? Well, he might have got himself a wife, and be well on the way towards extracting revenge, but, Emma wondered bleakly, how much joy did he expect to get out of either?

After dinner when Rick went out she decided to have an early night. He didn't say where he was going. He merely said briefly that he wouldn't be late and not to wait up for him. As he said that she had sensed the ironic glint in his eye, but she refused to look at him. Conversation during dinner had been difficult enough— she felt she just couldn't face any more of his taunting.

The next morning, after eating breakfast in their suite, they went out. The hotel was busy, but because it was so huge it gave the impression of being relatively quiet. Emma was glad to get away from it as she expected to bump into Blanche and Rex with every step she took, around every corner.

'You need more clothes,' said Rick, and while Emma thought wistfully of wandering along the Left Bank or around the famous flea or flower markets, to say nothing of having a great desire to visit the Louvre or Versailles again, he escorted her by taxi to one of the most expensive coiffeurs in the Champs-Elysées.

'Why do I have to come here?' she protested. 'I had my hair done in London

'It needs more attention, and so does your face,' was his far from flattering comment as, dismissing her sulky pleas adamantly, he turned to speak to the effusive proprietor. Emma was ignored while Rick, as usual, appeared to have no difficulty in commanding unlimited attention.

He would call for her at one, he said, leaving Emma gasping with dismay, as it was only ten o'clock.

By one she scarcely knew herself. Her hair and skin seemed to have undergone a miraculous transformation, and she had been assured many times that with a little care she would soon become quite irresistible.

To whom? she wondered, thinking unhappily of the stranger she had married. That Rick was rapidly beginning to prove irresistible to her was no proof that he would one day share her feelings. She would be much wiser to forget the nice things the staff of the salon had poured in her ears that morning and remember she was still plain Emma Davis.

Yet in spite of her doubts she couldn't help feeling a small thrill of satisfaction as she noticed Rick's brows rise a little when he first saw her. Her pleasure died, however, when his mouth tightened grimly, as if he couldn't decide whether her improved appearance was likely to prove an asset or a drawback. He should have thought of that before he'd taken her to Monsieur René's in the first place, shouldn't he?

Emma glanced at Rick quickly out of the corner of her eye, disappointed at his forbidding expression. 'Monsieur René said my bones are good.' Blatantly she found herself fishing for compliments when he didn't speak.

'Yes,' he nodded, without bothering to look at her again as he hailed another taxi.

He took her to a famous restaurant for lunch, where she ate oysters and sipped a dry white Burgundy without any feeling of awkwardness. She sensed the ease with which she was assuming her new role as his wife was surprising Rick too, and she wished vaguely that she had been able to explain how once she had been accustomed to living in a somewhat similar manner. But of course she could not. She had been away at school most of the time, but during the holidays her father had liked to take her around with him. He had never been as wealthy as Rick, though, and the excursions they had shared had more often been in the way of business rather than anything else.

After they had finished eating he escorted her to an equally famous fashion house on the Rue de la Paix. Again he left her after a brief consultation with the smiling vendeuse during which Emma heard him explaining that his wife required things they could take away almost immediately, that they had no time to spare for elaborate fittings. She would need, he instructed, among other things, a wardrobe suitable for the Caribbean. At this, Emma's heart sank. He must really intend taking her to his home and introducing her to his family. There was to be no escape, and her heart began pounding.

That evening, when Rick announced they would go down for dinner, Emma was glad she had included in her purchases a white silk dress. It was plain and youthfully discreet; there was nothing about it, she was sure, to make another woman green with envy. If Blanche were to see her in it, it would never arouse her animosity. Her sense of caution driving her one step farther, Emma screwed her hair tightly at the nape of her neck and used very little make-up. The results of all this effort was satisfying. While her hair might still gleam like pale, newly minted gold, the dragged-back style did nothing for her and her figure was, as yet, too thin to arouse a man's desire, to make anyone look twice. Or so she thought.

'Is that the best that damned shop could do?' Rick enquired sarcastically, eyeing Emma's scarcely impressive appearance with marked disfavour. 'God knows I'll be expected to pay through the nose for it.'

Innocently Emma nodded, saying nothing about the more décolleté models which required slight alterations but which she had been promised would be sent around to the hotel in the morning. 'You must let me graduate slowly, Rick. I'm not used to this kind of thing.'

'Yet you do have a kind of instinct for it, I've noticed,' he rejoined dryly, confirming her earlier suspicions. 'But then dangle a slice of the high life in front of any woman and most of them can't grab it quick enough—and take to it in the manner born.'

'Speaking from personal experience, I suppose,' she couldn't help retorting sharply, wondering unhappily just how many women he had spent that kind of money on? It wasn't the money so much as the implications of such transactions. It was something she felt curiously reluctant to face.

'Men usually have acquired some experience by my age,' he shrugged, glancing at her derisively, 'if that's all they have gained.'

He seemed to lose interest in the conversation after that and barely looked at her again as they went down in the lift to the restaurant. Emma hoped he didn't intend ignoring her all evening. She could have done with a little kinder attention as the thought of meeting Blanche held her as taut as a violin string. She was very tempted

to plead once more with Rick to leave, and had to warn
herself miserably that they did have a kind of contract,
and that any further move to break it must come from
him. She had said she would stay with him and stay she
must, until he chose to release her from her foolish
promises.

Her feelings somewhat mixed, that Rick didn't seem as
interested in her as he had done that morning at the hair-
dressers, Emma walked quietly by his side. It was what
she had planned, wasn't it? She had no right to feel hard
done by.

In the dining room there was no sign of Blanche, but in
a hotel the size of this, the chances of bumping into her
couldn't be great. If Emma had expected to feel relieved
by her cousin's non-appearance, she was doomed to disappointment. She soon began to feel more like a soldier in
a forest full of hidden enemies. She wished she could have
confronted Blanche at once and got it over with.

Rick, magnificent in evening dress, was formidably
silent and not disposed to linger. Watching him wistfully,
now and then, from under veiled lashes, Emma supposed
he looked nothing like a brand new bridegroom. He made
little effort to talk to her and the few attempts she made
to get a conversation going seemed to fall on deaf ears.
He looked irritated when one of the waiters had a surprised look in his eyes every time he called Emma *madame*,
but apart from this his face was as expressionless as usual.

'It's not my fault if he thinks I should still be
mademoiselle,' she said at last, wondering if it was. Colour
tinted her skin and she wished she hadn't spoken.

'Isn't it?' Rick rejoined irritably, but added nothing
more.

It was only just after ten when they went back upstairs.
Emma tried not to glance in the direction of the street, or
to envisage all the enchantment Paris had to offer after
dark. Night life, as such, held no great appeal for her, but

it might have been nice for once, especially on one's honeymoon. It must be heavenly to dance, or even wander on the banks of the Seine in the arms of a man one loved. Her heart gave a funny little bound as her eyes flickered uncertainly upwards to meet Rick's, only to find him staring at her in total indifference.

'Are you going out again?' she asked resignedly, as they reached their suite and he began pouring himself a drink.

'I might, in a few minutes,' he muttered curtly, as though wholly fed up with everything.

'There—there wasn't anyone downstairs,' she volunteered nervously, finding herself curiously reluctant to mention Blanche by name.

'We'll see,' he replied enigmatically.

She was about to ask what he meant when it was suddenly explained to her. There came a sharp rapping on the door, but when Rick called, '*Entrez,*' nothing happened.

Immediately startled, Emma gazed at him, but already he was striding over the room. A member of the hotel staff would have a key and would have obeyed Rick at once. So if it wasn't one of the staff—and they hadn't rung for anything—it could only be someone who knew them, perhaps another guest.

Although intuition warned Emma what to expect as Rick threw open the door, she couldn't restrain a horrified gasp as Blanche rushed in past him. There was no time for Emma to disappear, as she very much wished she could do.

Blanche was followed at a more leisurely pace by Rex Oliver, who looked the less disturbed of the two. Dazed, Emma stared numbly at them. What did Blanche want? What did she intend to say? Surely she wasn't going to try and bluff her way out? She could be convincingly ingenuous when she wanted to be, but Emma feared this time she wouldn't be good enough. Unfortunately, before she made a fool of herself, there was no chance to warn Blanche that Rick knew exactly what she'd been up to.

'Rick!' Blanche cried, turning, in one swift, graceful movement to clutch his arm. 'What a surprise, darling! What are you doing here? Why is Emma with you?' A poisonous little glance at Emma accompanied this last question.

'Why shouldn't she be?' Rick appeared to share none of Emma's uncertainty. His face was hard and he was arrogantly in charge of the situation. Staring coldly at Blanche, he explained, 'We were married yesterday.'

'M—married!' Emma had never heard Blanche stammer before and felt almost sorry for the other girl. Until Blanche laughed incredulously, 'Oh, don't be silly, darling, you can't be. You're engaged to me, remember? Not to—that silly little fool!'

'Something you forgot before I did.' His eyes full of contempt, Rick shook off her clinging hands as he glanced past her to Rex's lounging figure in the doorway.

'How can you say that?' Blanche exclaimed, her face slightly pink. 'I might be here with Rex, but you seem to be jumping to all the wrong conclusions. I'm just working for him.'

'You are?' Rick's smile was deceptive, for it contained no warmth. 'What job needs such close co-operation that you have to share a room?'

'You've been spying on me!' Blanche's temper, always uncontrollable, broke, although Emma saw she made a desperate effort to stay cool. 'Things aren't always what they seem. Rex . . .'

Rex merely shrugged at her pleading tones, realising the futility of the course she was attempting to pursue better than she did. 'I think the dice are too loaded against us, my dear. You gambled and lost, why not admit it?'

'I'm admitting nothing!' Blanche was quite magnificent, like a tigress at bay. Emma held her breath in momentary admiration and fear. Unfortunately Blanche turned on her. 'This is all your fault, you little slut! I might have known you'd let me down. As for you being married to Rick, I don't believe it!'

'It's quite true.' His face softening considerably, Rick reached an arm around Emma to draw her gently to his side. 'I've already told you. We were married in London yesterday morning.'

Blanche paused, staring, finding herself having reluctantly to re-think. Her thin mouth tightened to an ugly line. 'Are you trying to tell me you're in love?' she asked sarcastically, apparently convinced at last that Rick was telling the truth.

'A case of mutual attraction, strong enough to make us decide it would be a pity to waste a wedding ring,' Rick said smoothly.

'You came back from Australia sooner than you should have done!' Blanche accused him wildly.

'Yes, fortunately.' Rick's voice was still smooth, but Emma felt fury tightening the arm he had around her.

Frightened, she drew a deep breath, forgetting all about the promise she had made to pretend to be happily married. Instead of co-operating, she found herself pushing him away, her body so rigid that the others couldn't help but notice. 'Perhaps you should talk privately to Blanche, Rick, while I have a word with Rex? You could explain everything to her. Tell her how we're going to get a——'

'Emma!' Before she could say 'divorce', Rick shook her sharply, with a force which would have fooled no one. In a daze of dismay she saw Blanche's eyes narrow contemptuously and realised hollowly just how much she was letting Rick down.

'Have you nothing to say to your ex-lover?' Blanche enquired silkily of Emma, as Rick let her go. Blanche's shrewd mind was already at work on what she had quickly gathered from Emma's faltering statements. With a charmingly regretful smile she met Rick's eyes. 'Is it really necessary for us all to be heartbroken, darling? Perhaps, as Emma suggests, we should talk?'

'There's nothing to talk about,' he said icily.

'Your marriage needn't be permanent,' she pleaded. 'It was obviously on the rebound.'

Curtly he retorted. 'That's none of your business, Blanche.'

'If it isn't, why come here?' she cried. 'Don't tell me it was sheer coincidence that you picked this hotel for your honeymoon? If you're so much in love you can only see your—er—wife, why did you want to see me?'

'Please, Blanche . . .' Emma cut in, trying helplessly to stop the other girl from shouting the way she was doing. Surely there was such a thing as dignity?

'Shut up!'

Shrinking against the whiplash of Blanche's tongue, Emma felt forced to try again. 'With Rex gone . . .' she began, intending to say that when Rick had learnt this there had been nothing she could do to prevent him piecing together the whole story. Swiftly, though, Blanche stopped her.

'You were naturally too heartbroken to believe anything else mattered.'

Struck dumb again, Emma stared at her. Just what was Blanche trying to prove?

As Rick's mouth tightened ominously, Rex again intervened. 'It would be better for us all if we got out of here, Blanche. I think we've done enough damage as it is.' His eyes went quickly to Emma as he spoke and she realised bleakly the kind of construction Rick would place on his expression of silent pleading, especially when he added softly, 'I'm sorry, Emma. Words are rarely much good, but if Conway illtreats you, you must come to me.'

For a moment Emma thought Rick was going to hit

him and she clutched his arm frantically to stop him. 'Don't, Rick!' she cried, her face white.

Blanche, taking every advantage of an explosive situation, exclaimed sharply, 'Don't you see, Rick, she's terrified you might hurt him. You can see she's still crazy about him!'

Blanche was still shouting as Rex took her arm and literally dragged her out. Rick made no move to prevent them going. Indeed, his face was so black, Emma feared he was going to help them on their way. He must love Blanche very much if the sight of Rex and her together aroused such obvious feelings of jealousy and pain.

'This isn't the last you'll hear of me!' Blanche shrieked, as Rex closed the door.

When silence again reigned, Emma found she was trembling, but not so hard as she was when Rick reached her in two strides and grasped her shoulders. His hands would leave bruises in the morning, she thought dully, as his curt words ripped about her head.

'A fine help you proved to be!' he ground out, his eyes smouldering. 'You stood there shaking, looking as if you were about to faint. I might have known your feelings for Oliver would be stronger than your integrity. Nothing you owe me could compare with what you feel for that smarmy night club owner. Could it?'

'Rick, please! Rex isn't really like that. If you would only listen . . .' Emma was so upset she had no clear idea what she was saying. She only knew she must tell Rick the truth.

'He hadn't even the decency to offer you a word of apology,' Rick snarled, 'yet you're almost grovelling in his defence. I'd be a fool to have anything more to do with any of you!'

The flames of anger in his eyes burned her and his mouth was grim. Emma stared at him, her lips suddenly so dry she couldn't speak. Instinctively she was aware that if he was to learn the truth about her now, he really would send her away. One last deception uncovered would prove the last straw, and he wouldn't hesitate. Well, wasn't this what she wanted? No, she confessed to herself miserably, it wasn't. Apart from the fact that she had nowhere to go, she knew, with a lightning kind of illumination, that to lose Rick now would be like losing part of herself. It might be a strange way to feel about a man one hated, but she knew it was true. He had the power to make her heart race, as if she had been running. It could also make her limbs feel weak, even to recall being held in his arms. She wasn't sure of the extent of her involvement, nor had she any clear idea what was the matter with her? She only knew she couldn't let him go. One day, perhaps, but not yet.

'I'm tired,' she suddenly wrenched away from him. 'Look, Rick,' she said hoarsely, 'I'm sorry about Blanche and I can understand you feeling fed up, but is it my fault that neither of them appears to love either of us?'

'That wasn't the point!' he snarled savagely. 'The point is you let me down. You might be a rotten little actress, but you didn't even try. No one would have believed you were anything but a frightened adolescent. Maybe I should make sure no one will ever doubt you're a married woman again?'

Sensing his fury, Emma felt both nervous and terribly unhappy. He had been, she realised, in a vile temper since before they were married. It was what, she suspected, had driven him to such lengths in the first place, and what could drive him to even greater lengths if she didn't get out of his way very quickly.

'I—I think I'll go to bed. Goodnight, Rick.'

She was too late. Angry colour deepened over his hard cheekbones as he reached for her, before she could escape. Catching her off balance, as she turned, his arms grasped her as she stumbled against him. 'Maybe I can guess where I went wrong,' he muttered harshly, sweeping her off her feet.

His arms pinning her ruthlessly to him, he carried her swiftly over the lounge to her bedroom. As she struggled and gasped he threw her down on the bed with himself on top of her. Then, as if satisfied he had driven all the breath from her body, he eased his own body slightly away and began kissing her.

Emma wanted to resist him even while she knew she wanted him very much. Desperately she tried to hit out at him with her hands. She must try to ignore her burning, tormenting senses which tempted her to wait a few minutes before rejecting him. The frightening yet exciting dread that he might actually intend carrying out his angry threats fought with an instinctive horror of being taken in this way. If Rick had loved her it would have been different. She would still have been a little afraid, for it would have been her first time, but secure in his love she could have trusted him and asked him to be gentle. It was the lack of any sign of gentleness in the fierce possession of his mouth that warned her not to give in to him.

Yet his kisses were very hard to resist and she moaned as his mouth moved against her lips and throat. The neckline of her dress revealed the slight curve of her breasts and her breath caught as his seeking hands roved lightly over them. Then, with a quickness that stunned her, he drew down her zip and her dress was gone.

'Don't touch me!' she cried, wildly alarmed. 'Rick, please,' she gasped, as he took no notice, 'you can't take everything out on me!'

'Can't I?' he muttered, his teeth biting her naked shoulders, sending terrible tremors right down through her. 'Don't forget I bought you, so now I own you, which gives me more rights than Oliver ever had.'

'Forget about Rex,' she breathed chokingly. 'Think of Blanche, how much you love her.'

His mouth returned to hers but lightly so he could talk. 'I wanted her, but only as a suitable wife. Now I have another. If not quite so suitable,' he taunted, 'I'm quite willing to make the most of what I've got.'

Such insolence, at such a time, was beyond Emma, yet she tried to be calm. 'I shouldn't do anything you might regret in the morning.'

'I could regret doing nothing even more,' he muttered, smiling coolly as he increased the pressure of his mouth so she couldn't answer back.

If his smile had held anything but indifference she might have given in, but knowing how he hated her gave her the strength to fight him like a wildcat. Even so she soon found his powerful body, combined with the equally powerful forces of nature, proving too much for her. Weakly she began to moan as his sensual lips forced hers apart, holding her still until she became aflame with desire. His shirt was unbuttoned to the waist and she felt the impact of his flat, muscular stomach and wide powerful shoulders. His hands, she discovered, were as potent and expert as his mouth. Soon he had her head spinning with her senses until she scarcely knew where she was or what she was doing any more.

CHAPTER FIVE

RICK's hand moved slowly over her back before coming round to unhook the front of her bra. As one of the hooks caught her tender skin and she winced, he grunted curtly, 'God, you're as thin as a boy!'

Emma might have died with shame at his disparaging remark if she hadn't sensed his faint intrigue. Suddenly, as his hands continued moving over her, she felt his heart begin beating heavily. 'You must have something, if other men fancy you.'

This revolted her so much she began struggling again, trying to fight her way out of his arms as well as from the drugging effect of his lovemaking which threatened to overwhelm her. 'Rick!' she cried, 'You're mistaken. There's nothing about me.'

'Supposing you shut up and let me find out for myself?' he growled.

'No . . .' she pleaded brokenly, while suddenly finding it impossible to deny him any longer. As his mouth crushed punishingly down on hers, she found herself defeated as much by the strength of her own feelings as anything else. There was only her body held tightly against him and a hot, sweet tide of desire drawing her heedlessly on to meet the rising demand of his passion.

It was like a breath of cold air to become suddenly aware he had stopped kissing her. As he lifted his head she opened weighted eyes to find him watching her coldly. He was leaning over her, his eyes shuttered but intent on her hotly flushed face. Immediately fearing he was going away, Emma slid her arms up around his neck.

'Rick?' she whispered, 'I . . .'

'Do we have to talk?' he said hoarsely. 'You might

77

imagine you love Oliver, but he needn't be the only man in your life. You'll soon forget him.'

As soon as he mentioned Rex a terrible coldness came over her. It brought back Blanche's accusing expression too vividly, making Emma feel guilty and uncomfortable to even be in the same building. 'Blanche and Rex must still be here,' she exclaimed, her face paling with apprehension.

Her distress checked Rick at once. 'So he still matters that much!' His eyes darkening with anger, he threw her away from him, getting up from the bed. 'You little fool, you're as much in love with him as ever!'

The crash of the door behind him did nothing to prevent Emma's tears. It hurt that he hadn't stopped to hear her explanation, but it was perhaps just as well. She had been about to tell him how uneasy she felt with Blanche and Rex in the hotel and had been going to suggest she wouldn't mind leaving immediately and going somewhere else. Now she could only feel thankful that Rick's quick temper and even swifter reactions had prevented her from making such a humiliating and impulsive request. That he believed her to love Rex might prove her only real means of protection against him. What did a little pain now matter if it enabled her to escape even greater heartache in the future?

Emma didn't know if Rick went out again after he left her. She thought he must have done, for the suite was very quiet. It took her a long time to get to sleep and when she woke her head was aching terribly. So were her shoulders. That, she soon realised, was because Rick was shaking her.

'Wake up,' he spoke tersely. 'We're leaving.'

'Leaving?' Startled, she twisted from his harsh grasp and stared at him, 'Now? Today?'

'This morning.'

She saw he was watching her curiously and her face

flushed as she became aware she was naked. Last night, after he left her, she had been too miserable to bother finding something to put on, and the bedroom was warm enough. Now she wished she had.

Knowing Rick was indifferent helped, as she slipped back under the sheets. 'Why have we to leave in such a hurry?' she protested, and almost sighed at her own contrariness. Last night she had wanted to leave as quickly as possible.

'Put something on and I'll tell you,' he rejoined curtly.

'If you turn round,' she shivered at something in his eyes, 'I'll get my dressing-gown.'

'Do we have to play such games?' he snapped. 'What if I don't?'

'Oh, I don't suppose it would matter,' she made a great effort to achieve a kind of sophisticated casualness. 'I don't have that kind of effect on you.'

'What about last night?' he drawled, his eyes suddenly speculative.

Emma swallowed. 'Well, we both knew that was frustration over Blanche. Otherwise you wouldn't have touched me.'

'Possibly you're right,' he agreed, turning around.

Scrambling quickly out of bed, reaching for her dressing-gown, she failed to realise he had turned immediately back again and was appraising her slight figure. When she discovered it the pink in her cheeks deepened, but she felt too numb to really care. She had no idea the indifference she felt was due to delayed shock, as the events of the previous evening caught up with her. She was only conscious, from the look on Rick's dark face, that he concluded she was quite used to parading in front of men with little on and saw no real reason why she should make an exception of her husband.

Her suspicions seemed correct when Rick spoke. 'I expect Oliver has seen you like this many times?'

She tied the sash on her robe tightly, not caring for the dangerous glint in his eyes. 'What—what makes you think that?'

'Don't try me too far,' he shot back, his mouth cruel. Then he shrugged his broad shoulders. 'What the hell does it matter? I didn't come here to discuss your past lovers. I came to tell you we're leaving for home.'

'Home?'

'Barbados. I was a fool to come here at all and I don't intend staying a moment longer than I have to. Not now. We're booked on the morning flight, which gives us just over an hour.'

There had been too many shocks over the past few days in Emma's young life, for one more to prove her undoing, but she felt oddly reluctant to accompany Rick to his island home. Feeling unable to face anything more, she hunted around for excuses. 'My new clothes? The saleswoman said they would be delivered.'

'Trust a woman to think of clothes first, but they're already here. Paris was awake and at work some hours ago.'

'That's all right, then,' she faltered, not having the nerve to say, after making a fuss, that it was unimportant. Knowing she could no longer put off what was really important, she asked reluctantly, 'Won't Blanche want to know more than you told her last night? Perhaps you should see her? Or she might come to see you?'

'That's what I'm afraid of.'

'Well then . . .'

'If you aren't ready in five minutes,' he cut in threatening, 'you'll come as you are. I have no desire to see Blanche again, or for some time, anyway. While you, I'm afraid, as a married woman, must learn to forget about other men.'

'How many do you think I've had?' she whispered painfully.

'Don't tell me,' Rick held up a decisive hand. 'I dislike being given information which I've no means of checking.'

'I see,' she sighed, a lump in her throat as she wished futilely that he could have trusted her. But even if he came to like her he might never bring himself to do that.

'While you're taking your shower,' Rick advised stringently, ignoring her despondent face, 'I'll bring in the parcels that came. After you find something to wear, pack the rest. Don't waste any more time or I'll come and do it for you.'

Unable to bear even the thought of him manhandling the new, delicate underwear she liked so much, Emma almost fell over herself to do as she was told. Swiftly she showered, then extracted from the pile of things Rick had tipped ruthlessly on her bed, a pair of thin trousers and a silky top with a matching waistcoat. What was left she thrust in her two lightweight suitcases and after running a quick comb through her thick hair she slung a large, soft shoulder bag over her slim shoulders and was ready.

They travelled first class from France. It was a long flight and although Emma appreciated the extra comfort she grew restless long before they arrived at Barbados. There were quite a few men in the first-class cabin, but not many women. The men looked mostly like business executives and she was surprised to find several of them glancing at her with interest. She didn't understand how her extreme slimness gave her a kind of understated elegance which, with her shining fair hair, was very attractive. She simply thought the attention she was receiving was because she was so young. Sometimes, when Rick glanced at her, she felt more convinced than ever that her lack of years irritated him a lot, although he didn't actually comment on it again.

As the sky lightened and brightened as they flew farther west, Emma knew a grim tremor of apprehension. What

were Rick's family like? She hadn't been curious before.
Now she wanted to know everything.

'Is your father alive, Rick?' she asked.

He was sitting beside her studying figures on sheets of
paper, but she considered her lack of knowledge concern-
ing him more important.

'No,' he replied, without looking up.

'You did mention your stepmother,' she persisted, 'but
you haven't told me anything about her.'

He slanted her a quick glance, then with a sigh laid his
papers aside. 'Tell me exactly what it is you want to
know,' he said resignedly.

His manner was enough to put anyone off. Frowning,
Emma stared at him, biting her lip, suddenly at a loss when
thus challenged. Having decided a few cool little questions
were all that was necessary she was impatient to find herself
floundering in a manner far from as precise as she had
planned. 'If—if we'd been an—a normal married couple,
I'd have known, wouldn't I?'

'You'd have known,' he smiled, so oddly teasing that
she flushed, realising vaguely he wasn't speaking of his
relations. 'You haven't much figure,' he went on, almost
absently, as he studied her, 'but your skin is beautiful.'

'I wasn't talking about me, or my skin,' she stammered,
brushing aside his remarks indignantly while trying to
staunch the little flame which was spreading through her.

'I was only saying how parts of you leave nothing to be
desired,' he protested idly.

Only you don't desire me, she almost retorted, but when
her colour deepened warmly he seemed able to read her
mind. His unusually light mood persisting, he reached
over unexpectedly, pulling her to him. Then bending his
head he gently kissed the soft sheen of her bare neck,
where she had left her blouse open. 'You smell nice.
Delectable,' he mused, trailing mocking fingers down her
arm, as he lowered his head again.

For the moment they appeared to have the corner of the cabin to themselves, most of the other occupants having disappeared up the funny little spiral staircase to the free upstairs bar. Emma shivered, as the flames Rick ignited fanned to a fire and she shrank defensively away from him. 'Leave me alone, Rick,' she whispered, turning her head from the searching pressure of his lips. If he didn't she couldn't be sure of her own reactions. She had a disturbing desire to put her arms around him and beg him to hold her close.

'Pity my name isn't Oliver,' he said curtly, drawing back in his seat. 'Air travel arouses curious emotions.'

'At least Rex likes me better than you do.' She felt very agitated, and wasn't even thinking of Rex.

'Don't let anyone hear you saying things like that,' Rick warned darkly.

'I wanted to talk about your family,' she reminded him tautly.

'Oh, what the hell,' he muttered grimly, but after a slight pause he obliged, explaining that as well as a stepmother he had also a stepbrother and sister.

When Emma glanced at him doubtfully, he said dryly, 'Don't worry too much. Rita isn't so very difficult to get on with. She married my father a couple of years before he died. Gail and Ben were in their early teens and occasionally they've been a handful, but I think they're shaping up all right now.'

'How long is it since your father died?'

'Ten years.'

So Rick must have been partly responsible, at least, for the upbringing of the children. Emma didn't doubt he would undertake such a responsibility as he would anything else he considered his duty. Nothing might prove too much for him to take on. Already she was beginning to notice how authority sat easily on his broad shoulders.

'Do—do you all still live together?' she asked next.

'When I'm in Barbados it's convenient and when I'm not they're there to keep an eye on the house.'

'And—and now?'

'Now?' His brows rose and his eyes glinted with their familiar cynical hardness. 'Now makes no difference, my dear girl, if you mean because I'm married and you'll be there. In a year we split up. I certainly don't intend interrupting either my family's routine or my own for the sake of someone who's only going to be with us a few months.'

It was evening when they landed at the Grantley Adams International Airport, eleven miles from Bridgetown, the capital of Barbados. Relieved to be off the plane, Emma stood sniffing the air like an eager young puppy. It was a lovely evening, the air balmy, not unlike Paris, yet different. It took her scarcely more than a few seconds to realise it was more exotic, in a tropical kind of way. It seemed to contain the scent of a thousand flowers and trees. The slight breeze whispered of things she knew nothing about, but something stirred in her blood, quickening her pulse as she felt herself responding. Somewhere in the background she heard the beat of a steel band and thought of limbo dancing and calypso singing under starry skies on a beautiful West Indian night. She thought of Rick by her side, dancing with her dreamily, holding her gently, then more urgently as the music grew wilder and heightened their awareness of each other.

As she quivered visibly, Rick turned, speaking curtly as he noticed her dreamy expression. 'Snap out of it, Emma. I don't have all night, and if you're trying to impress me you're wasting both my time and your own.'

'Impress you?' she faltered, coming back to earth with the bump he no doubt intended.

'Did you think you could get round me by pretending you imagined you'd landed in paradise?' he snapped sarcastically.

'I wasn't pretending,' she gulped, 'neither was I trying to impress you.'

'Weren't you?' he shrugged, so totally disbelieving that she was convinced he was being deliberately unkind and getting some sadistic pleasure from it.

They were met by a car driven by a coloured Barbadian called Belasco, who greeted Rick as Boss but appeared much more interested in Emma.

'New missus, boss?' he asked.

'Yes,' Rick introduced them and Emma smiled, feeling a little happier than she had done since Rick's cruel remarks. Surprisingly Belasco appeared to be looking at her with approval and she sensed she had at least made one friend.

They travelled north, towards Speightstown, where Rick informed her briefly most of the sugar plantations were to be found. To Emma the countryside was beautiful, with orchards of lemon and orange trees along with avocadoes and bananas and hosts of others she failed to recognise. She would liked to have asked Rick about some of the things she saw but dared not risk another rebuff like the one she had suffered at the airport. Then she had felt hurt tears stinging the back of her eyes and she guessed how scathing his remarks would be if she gave in to them and broke down completely.

Turning her eyes from the enticing views on either side, she caught sight of Belasco's curious face in the driving miror. It wasn't until then that it suddenly struck her that Rick's people would surely be expecting him to bring home a beautiful bride. If Belasco could look surprised by her plainness, how much more so would Rick's family be?

Emma's face was visibly paler as she stepped out of the car in front of a wonderful old colonial-style mansion. 'Is—is this all yours?' she breathed, in an agonised whisper.

'Just one of those things you'll have to try to get used

to.' His voice was curt, but his eyes were a little kinder as he understood she wasn't used to living in a house like this. He had to spoil it all by adding derisively, 'It's much easier to become addicted to wealth than poverty. Just as long as you remember you only have a year.'

'It—it isn't your wealth,' she dismissed that, for hadn't she discovered it was perfectly possible to live without it, 'and you don't need to keep on repeating that I only have a year—I heard the first time and I don't want any longer. It's what your family are going to think.'

'Meaning?'

'They'll be expecting someone quite different from me. Someone beautiful.'

'Well, work on it,' he drawled carelessly. 'You never know what you might achieve. A lot of lovely women look far from pretty first thing in the morning.'

How did he know? Unhappily Emma stared at him, but obviously thinking she was still thinking of his family, Rick sighed shortly. 'They aren't ogres, you know, and a plain girl might just happen to be more acceptable than a beautiful one, women being what they are.'

'You obviously being an authority?' she was stung to retort.

'I've known plenty,' he admitted dryly.

Plenty who would have been only too willing to become Mrs Rick Conway, she guessed, with sudden insight, her unhappiness curiously deepening.

Leaving Belasco unloading their luggage they went into the house. Emma followed Rick silently as she saw he was clearly impatient with the conversation they had been having and had no intention of discussing the matter further. As they entered the impressive hall, a woman and a girl came out of one of the rooms and crossed the cool tiled floor towards them.

'Rick darling!' the woman exclaimed, 'we didn't look for you as soon as this.

Bending, he kissed the woman's smoothly made up cheek lightly, then the girl's in the same manner, before he caught Emma's hand, drawing her forward.

'This is Emma,' he said coolly. 'Emma, meet my stepmother and my stepsister Gail.' He didn't explain why he had returned sooner than he had apparently intended.

Emma was very aware of Rita's appraising eyebrows, her speculative stare. 'Forgive me, Rick, but I thought it was Blanche.'

'So it was, but I changed my mind and married her cousin instead,' he said, as though there was nothing out the ordinary in such a statement. Drawing Emma nearer, he tightened his arm around her waist. 'I hope you'll do your best to make Emma feel at home.'

Or else, his enigmatic expression seemed to say, but in such an impersonal way that Emma knew it would be unwise to feel comforted.

Rita gave little away either. 'Have you had dinner?' she asked, in the manner of a woman who clearly needed time to think things over.

'Shall I ring?' asked Gail, obviously finding it impossible to evoke any interest in Rick's surprisingly quiet little wife and looking for a means of escape.

'No,' said Rick, 'we ate on the plane. Perhaps a snack, but we can have it later.'

'I'll arrange it,' Rita smiled, like someone who considered the opposition didn't stand a chance.

Indifferently Rick nodded. Without letting go of Emma he guided her upstairs, but once in the spacious bedroom which was to be hers, he let go of her abruptly.

'All right?' he asked, and when she said yes, he exclaimed coldly, 'We have communicating rooms, for appearances' sake. The usual door in between which naturally I won't use. You can have the bathroom, I'll use one of those on the corridor.'

Which ensured her complete privacy but meant she wouldn't be seeing him after they retired. He spoke so politely he might have been passing the time of day with a stranger, or an unwelcome guest.

'Are you disappointed?' he read her bewildered face, jeering at her unconscious thoughts.

'No. Why should I be?' Emma forced herself to ask coolly.

His dark brows rose, frankly cynical. 'You didn't imagine I was planning to amuse myself with Oliver's cast-offs, did you? If I've occasionally kissed you, don't jump to the wrong conclusions. You can, I admit, provoke me. Your mouth is very kissable, if nothing else.'

'How do you mean—nothing else?' Emma stared at him mutinously.

'I mean, it's not so innocent. You've been around.'

Seeing red at his insolence, she exclaimed, 'I suppose none of the women you've been out with have been around? Do you demand written evidence of a spotless character?'

'You little brat,' his eyes smouldered, 'I don't need that kind of evidence. A man can usually tell. And while I might have taken other women out, this is the first time I've ever married one of them.'

'You aren't congratulating yourself, though,' Emma choked. 'Only your temper drove you to marry me.'

'Too true,' he grated tersely. 'Now I wish to hell I hadn't. I should have offered other things, like Oliver did with you and Blanche. We could have gone to Paris without being married.'

'At least,' Emma cried, 'Rex is rarely a hypocrite!'

Swiftly he grasped her arm, his fingers steel-like and hurting. 'You'll apologise for that,' his face was suddenly taut with fury. 'I don't take insults from either men or women. Apologise or else!'

He looked so arrogant she quite believed the warning

in his voice was no idle threat. All the same, she continued to defy him. 'I won't,' she said, 'because it's the truth.'

'If you don't,' he murmured suavely, 'I know how to make you change your tune. The bed, for instance, is only two feet away.'

'You wouldn't dare!' she breathed, her face paling, then flooding with colour as she visualised exactly how he would punish her there. It made her tremble even to think of it. An apology might be infinitely preferable to that. 'I'm sorry,' she mumbled, tearing her eyes away from his darkly handsome face.

'That's better,' he said succinctly.

'I—I hate you,' she whispered, the taste in her mouth so bitter she felt sick.

'Don't be too sure of it,' he drawled mockingly, turning from her abruptly. 'I'll see you downstairs in half an hour,' he added.

As the door closed behind him, Emma collapsed on the bed. Feeling unbelievably exhausted, she allowed salty tears to overflow and scald her cold cheeks. Forcibly, she had to remind herself that she had no one but herself to blame for the poor opinion Rick had of her. But it still hurt to know that it was only because he believed her a low creature to be despised that she was here. If she gave in to her deepening desire to tell him the truth, he would send her home. True, he had married her as much to salve his own pride as anything else. Yet she suspected he wouldn't allow that to deter him from what he might consider his duty if he were to learn she was innocent of most of the crimes he thought her guilty of.

Suddenly, as a wave of homesickness engulfed her, she was tempted to go to him and confess everything. Sadly she found herself yearning for the familiar green fields, the rain and the grey English skies. Nostalgically she even thought of Daisy's large brown eyes searching for the girl who had always looked after her so gently. As Emma sat thinking about the farm her tears flowed faster. It pained her that she hadn't been able to say a proper goodbye. On top of this was the worry of not knowing how Hilda and old Jim were managing without her. Blanche was unlikely to be of much help. Besides, her mood would be far from co-operative by the time she got home.

Sighing, Emma scrubbed the tears from her face before stepping out of her clothes to get under the shower. It was no use worrying now, but she wished the last few days hadn't happened so quickly. If she had been given time to consider sensibly just what she had been about to embark on, she doubted if she would have been here tonight.

Half an hour later, neatly dressed in a light print dress, she met Rick's family again, and this time Gail's brother. A good-looking, rather brash young man of twenty-five, he brightened when he caught sight of Emma.

'Thank heavens!' he grinned as Rick, a watchful step behind Emma, introduced her. 'I wasn't looking forward to meeting Rick's model girl—they're too liable to scream at one hair out of place, but I do feel I might get to like you.'

If Emma was rather startled by his somewhat tactless approach, Rick ignored it. 'Get Emma a drink, Ben,' he said, 'and one for me. I'm glad you managed to make it.'

Rita was speaking to a servant, Gail was fishing through a pile of cassettes. Seemingly unperturbed by his stepbrother's sarcasm, Ben poured them all drinks and returned. He passed Emma hers, his eyes still studying her.

'She has a rather old-fashioned look, like her name. Sort of chaste . . .'

'There's nothing old-fashioned about my wife,' Rick replied sardonically, 'but don't go making her worse than she is.'

While Emma flushed unhappily at what seemed a

veiled insult, another servant entered with a laden trolley.

'I thought, if it was only a snack you wanted, you might as well have it here.' Rita, dismissing the servants, smiled charmingly at Rick, who nodded his assent.

Rita, still attractive at sixty, turned, her face sobering coldly as she glanced at Emma. 'If you sat over there, my dear, you might manage your drink better.'

Emma gave a start, having almost forgotten she was holding anything. She was dismayed to find the greeny liquid, whatever it was, trickling over her hand as the glass tilted. 'I—I'm sorry,' she faltered, her eyes wide with distress.

'Perhaps you had too much on the plane?' Gail quipped with a malicious giggle.

'Yes—No. I don't really think so . . .' Emma stammered, wondering miserably why Rick made no attempt to help her. He actually looked as though he enjoyed seeing her being got at.

'Sit down, can't you,' he said impatiently, giving the impression he would support Rita rather than his wife.

Meekly Emma did as she was told. Rita, busy dispensing coffee, spoke again, with audacious sharpness. 'I hope you're going to fit in, my dear. There are a lot of parties and that kind of thing—a lot of social life on the island. Otherwise you're going to be very bored.'

Almost as if she were a stranger and must remain one. Confused, Emma stared into Rita's icy eyes, again wondering why Rick didn't come to her rescue. Rita was making it quite clear she had no intention of handing over the reins of the household, certainly not into the hands of an incompetent teenager.

A flicker of devilment in Emma prompted her to say smoothly, 'I'm not all that fond of parties. I expect,' deliberately she allowed her eyes to travel round, 'I'll find more important things to occupy my time here.'

Rita's thin mouth tightened. 'Rick likes his household managed properly and I'm used to his ways.'

About to reassert herself more strongly, Emma suddenly subsided. Why bother? Wasn't she only Rick's wife for a year? He wouldn't want her even pretending to be mistress here. The best thing she could do was to leave it all to Rita, who apparently had every intention of carrying on as usual. Then, when she went, it would just be as if a faint breeze had come and gone.

'You do like meeting people, I suppose?' Rita, like all bullies, trampled even harder when her victim made no further protest.

Emma said carefully, 'Of course.'

'She won't be meeting many for a while.' Rick spoke at last, and firmly.

Emma winced, strangely having more regard for his opinion than for Rita's. He must think she wouldn't know how to conduct herself in front of his fine friends.

'I did promise Veronica you would be at the party she's giving tomorrow night, Rick,' Rita frowned. 'She was so persistent I hardly liked to refuse.'

'She doesn't waste much time,' Ben said dryly.

His mother ignored him as she went on speaking to Rick. 'She had heard you were coming back, and you know how it is with her.'

'Sometimes it's almost too obvious.' Rick's face hardened and Emma thought he was going to say more. Instead, he shrugged. 'This once we might oblige, but I have too much to catch up on to waste time over too many social functions.'

Rita said thoughtfully, 'You don't usually say no to a party, when you're at home, especially Veronica's.'

That Rita was doing her best to ignore Rick's marriage stood out a mile, and Emma winced. Who was this mysterious Veronica, whom Rita apparently favoured more than herself?

'Rick was saying, 'I want to go over the whole estate as soon as possible.'

Why was that? Emma glanced enquiringly at Rick, but he wasn't looking at her. He began talking to Rita of other things, and both Rita and Gail seemed happy to follow his lead and ignore her. Emma swallowed a surge of resentment as she remembered his lectures on keeping up appearances. He was doing absolutely nothing to help if he wanted to give the impression that they were a happily married couple.

Ben was the only one who seemed to appreciate her presence and during the next few weeks Emma was to become grateful for his kindness and his company.

The following evening arrived all too soon. Emma had seen little of Rick all day, but while she missed him there was plenty to distract her attention. The house was old but had been modernised and was large and extremely comfortable. It was surrounded by extensive grounds and beyond these lay acres of gently rolling sugar cane.

The gardens were extensive, keeping the sugar cane at bay, and Emma was impressed by the sheer beauty of the landscape. As she was interested in farming, the cultivation of the estate intrigued her and she would have liked to have asked Rick about it, but he wasn't around. He was busy, Rita told her when she asked where he was, while her scornful glance seemed to add that a new bride shouldn't have to look far for her husband.

Rather than suffer further humiliation, Emma wandered about on her own, and it was Ben who answered her many questions about the island, its people and the sugar plantations. She had found the huge swimming pool in the gardens and decided to avail herself of it as she was hot and sticky from her wanderings. She had been in and was out, sitting on the edge of it when Ben found her.

'Rick not with you?' he grinned, dropping down beside her.

'As you can see,' she said shortly.

'Never mind,' he went on smiling idly. 'He's busy. I've been with him all morning,' he groaned ruefully, 'and he never stops.'

Emma glanced at him curiously. 'Don't you like being busy?'

Ben shrugged. 'Sometimes. Oh, most of the time, I suppose, but there are limits, and Rick's a slave-driver. I did think he would slow up a bit for you. You may not be a model, but you're a sweet young thing. I can't think what he's thinking about.'

Emma flushed unhappily but tried to make light of it. 'Other things, apparently.'

'Well, if he neglects you, you don't want to let him get away with it.'

'Or he'll treat you the same as he does all the others,' another voice finished for him.

Turning with a gasp, Emma found Gail staring down on her. She hadn't heard her approach and she flinched from the other girl's callously presented warning. While Ben's words had been lightly teasing, his sister's held more than a hint of deliberate spite.

CHAPTER SIX

FLASHING a disapproving glance at his sister, Ben placed a comforting hand over Emma's, as it lay beside him. 'Don't take any notice,' he smiled. 'Gail is one of this world's little cats. She can't help her claws.'

Can't she? Emma thought derisively, withdrawing her hand.

'You'll have to watch Veronica this evening,' Gail continued, undeterred. 'She and Rick have been close for ages. She might have been reconciled to your glamorous cousin, but she'll never understand what attracted Rick to you.'

'Emma isn't plain. She's too thin, but she's quite pretty,' Ben insisted kindly.

Gail merely raised pencilled brows. 'Well, her story has to be interesting, if she's not.'

Because Gail's eyes were so speculative, Emma's face burnt. Scrambling to her feet, she dived in the pool again. Having guessed what was coming she had no wish to satisfy Gail's curiosity as to exactly how she and Rick had met and married.

Floating on her back, letting the water gently soothe her, she soon felt a little better. Faintly she could hear Ben and Gail quarrelling, but was too far away to make out what they were saying to each other. She could see she would have to grow a thicker skin if she was to survive here for the next few months. Rita and Gail obviously disliked her, and she couldn't expect any help from Rick. Added to this would probably be the animosity of his former girl-friends. Only Ben was inclined to be kind, and again she felt a warm surge of gratitude. If she ever needed it, perhaps he would help her.

Veronica Ray lived several miles down the coast with her two brothers, Miles and Harley. The family owned a large business in Bridgetown and made enough money to give Veronica most of the things her rather mercenary soul craved. That her brothers hadn't been able to capture Rick Conway for her was something Veronica held against them. Yet, at the party she gave, the surprise on her face, on meeting Rick's young wife, might have informed the least intelligent of onlookers that she was filled with new hope.

Emma, not slow to read Veronica's mind, felt, as the evening progressed, that the other girl might have good reason to be so flagrantly sure of herself. As she watched them dancing, she noticed Rick's slow, appreciative smile as he gazed down into Veronica's velvet-dark eyes. Emma he almost ignored all evening, and his neglect was beginning to make her feel desperately uncomfortable. When a bride of just a few days was ignored by her husband, this could only become a subject of malicious gossip, especially in such a closely knit community.

She turned with almost visible relief when Ben asked her to dance. 'Oh, thank you,' she murmured, a glimmer of tears in her eyes.

'Don't tell me you and Rick have really fallen out?' he teased. His voice was light, but Emma could see he was slightly puzzled by the way Rick was behaving.

When she shook her fair head, he clearly wasn't satisfied. 'I wasn't serious, this morning. Rick can be a devil at times, but he's usually quick to forgive. Besides,' he smiled, 'most new husbands are inclined to be extremely tolerant.'

'Because we're married it doesn't mean he has to be glued to my side!' Emma protested feebly.

'Still no valid reason for neglecting you, my child.'

Wishing everyone wouldn't insist on calling her that, she retorted a little too fiercely, 'I don't expect him to neglect his friends.'

Say Hello to Yesterday

Holly Weston had done it all alone.

She had raised her small son and worked her way up to features writer for a major newspaper. Still the bitterness of the the past seven years lingered.

She had been very young when she married Nick Falconer—but old enough to lose her heart completely when he left. Despite her success in her new life, her old one haunted her.

But it was over and done with—until an assignment in Greece brought her face to face with Nick, and all she was trying to forget....

Time of the Temptress

The game must be played his way!

Rebellion against a cushioned, controlled life had landed Eve Tarrant in Africa. Now only the tough mercenary Wade O'Mara stood between her and possible death in the wild, revolution-torn jungle.

But the real danger was Wade himself—he had made Eve aware of herself as a woman.

"I saved your neck, so you feel you owe me something," Wade said. "But you don't owe me a thing, Eve. Get away from me." She knew she could make him lose his head if she tried. But that wouldn't solve anything....

Your Romantic Adventure Starts Here.

Born Out of Love

It had to be coincidence!

Charlotte stared at the man through a mist of confusion. It was Logan. An older Logan, of course, but unmistakably the man who had ravaged her emotions and then abandoned her all those years ago.

She ought to feel angry. She ought to feel resentful and cheated. Instead, she was apprehensive—terrified at the complications he could create.

"We are not through, Charlotte," he told her flatly. "I sometimes think we haven't even begun."

Man's World

Kate was finished with love for good.

Kate's new boss, features editor Eliot Holman, might have devastating charms—but Kate couldn't care less, even if it was obvious that he was interested in her.

Everyone, including Eliot, thought Kate was grieving over the loss of her husband, Toby. She kept it a carefully guarded secret just how cruelly Toby had treated her and how terrified she was of trusting men again.

But Eliot refused to leave her alone, which only served to infuriate her. He was no different from any other man...or was he?

These FOUR free Harlequin Presents novels allow you to enter the world of romance, love and desire. As a member of the Harlequin Home Subscription Plan, you can continue to experience all the moods of love. You'll be inspired by moments so real... so moving... you won't want them to end. So start your own Harlequin Presents adventure by returning the reply card below. <u>DO IT TODAY!</u>

TAKE THESE 4 BOOKS AND TOTE BAG FREE!

Mail to: Harlequin Reader Service
1440 South Priest Drive, Tempe, AZ 85281

YES, please send me FREE and without obligation my 4 **Harlequin Presents**
If you do not hear from me after I have examined by 4 FREE books, please send me the 6 new **Harlequin Presents** each month as soon as they come off the presses. I understand that I will be billed only $10.50 for all 6 books. There are no shipping and handling nor any other hidden charges. There is no minimum number of books that I have to purchase. In fact, I can cancel this arrangement at any time. The first 4 books and the tote bag are mine to keep as FREE gifts, even if I do not buy any additional books. CP186

NAME	(please print)	

ADDRESS		APT. NO.

CITY	STATE	ZIP

Signature (If under 18, parent or guardian must sign).

BUSINESS REPLY CARD

First Class Permit No. 70 Tempe, AZ

POSTAGE WILL BE PAID BY ADDRESSEE

Harlequin Reader Service
1440 South Priest Drive
Tempe, Arizona 85266

EXTRA BONUS
MAIL YOUR ORDER
TODAY AND GET A
FREE TOTE BAG
FROM HARLEQUIN.

'It's just possible his friends might understand,' Ben retorted dryly, not for a moment fooled by the shimmer in Emma's eyes.

'Oh, never mind!' she made an effort to speak naturally, to dismiss Rick from her thoughts. 'I like dancing, and you're good.'

'So are you,' he laughed, whirling her in his arms in such a way as made her almost forget the idle tongues, the quick, speculative glances which clearly wondered what on earth Rick Conway had seen in her.

Ben danced with her three times before leaving reluctantly to dance with another girl. 'I'll be back,' he assured her. 'You're really something. I can't remember when I've enjoyed anything so much.'

Rick was dancing with Veronica again and Rita and Gail were nowhere to be seen. Again Emma sat by herself with no one taking any notice, her face so stiff from trying to retain a happy expression that it soon felt completely frozen. Rick did, she saw, eventually dance with someone else, another lovely girl, with whom he was soon dancing cheek to cheek. The girl had her arms around his neck, and had pulled him down to her.

When numbly Emma turned her head away, it was to encounter Veronica's malignant stare.

'It hardly looks as if you're going to be able to hold him, honey. I'll give you a few weeks at the most.'

Emma replied with difficulty, 'Rick and I understand each other.'

'I wish I did!' said Veronica, with sharp laughter, as she sailed away.

Emma was never sure how she got through the rest of the evening. Rick asked her to dance once and she refused, she felt so sick. He had taken her in to supper but barely spoken to her. She told herself she was relieved when he left her while knowing she would have given anything to have danced with him and kept him by her side.

Tossing and turning later in her huge lonely bed, with the scent of jasmine and gardenias floating in through the open window, she found it difficult to sleep. Eventually, when she did, it was to dream she was in Rick's arms and he was holding her close. A slight smile flitted across Emma's tear-wet cheeks as she kissed him and clung to him feverishly.

Neither Rita nor Gail appeared to come down for breakfast, for it was the second morning that they hadn't been there. Rick wasn't there either and the housekeeper told her he was out on the plantation.

'He works very hard,' the Bajan woman said.

'I thought he had a manager?' Emma carefully sipped her coffee. The rolls were fresh and she made herself butter one, although she didn't feel hungry. She declined the offer of anything cooked.

'Yes, the boss has a manager. He's a good man, and then there's Mr Ben. He's leaving, of course. Going to manage his own plantation, one day.'

'Is he looking forward to it?' Emma enquired, looking anxious.

'Of course!' the housekeeper beamed. 'Mr Rick says he can go as soon as he's learnt enough.'

Emma bit her lip. She liked Ben, she hoped he wouldn't disappear too soon. Uncertainly she glanced at the housekeeper, who was still hovering. Normally, she knew, she would be expected to take over the duties of a mistress, but apart from the fact that Rick had never asked her to, she realised it would be a waste of time. And she had no intention of upsetting Rita, who would have to look after Rick when she was gone.

Fearing the woman was on the point of asking whose orders she was to take, now that the boss was married, Emma finished her coffee hastily and went out. 'I'll go and see if I can find anyone,' she said.

In spite of her endeavours, she didn't see Rick all day,

and by evening she was seething with unhappy resentment that he was so obviously avoiding her. Heedless of anything but her own anger, she recklessly threw open the double doors between their rooms when she heard him moving about.

'Yes, what is it?' he asked sharply, clearly surprised as he paused in the act of unbuttoning his shirt.

Wrenching her startled eyes from his hair-darkened chest, she saw he was looking strangely tired. Imagining this must be partly due to the attention he had paid other women, the night before, only increased her sense of grievance. Without hesitation she accused him, 'You talked of having to keep up appearances! You said I must pretend to be a loving wife! Well, how can I when you practically ignore my existence?'

Coolly he regarded her. 'I've changed my mind, I'm afraid. What's the use of fawning over each other when it doesn't mean anything? This way, when we part company, we won't have to invent fictitious explanations. No one will look for them as they'll have been predicting a break-up from the beginning.'

Emma's anger was changing rapidly to misery. 'You have it all worked out?'

'Don't look so bitter,' he returned dryly. 'You've known from the start what was to happen. You didn't go into this with your eyes shut.'

'No, I didn't, did I?' she agreed dully.

'Perhaps,' his voice hardened, 'you're hoping to secure a permanent niche for yourself? Now that you've seen the way I live.'

Emma's face went white. 'No!' she choked. 'How could I, when you don't even like me?'

'All the same,' he rejoined grimly, 'you'll conduct yourself in a reasonable manner, while you're here.'

'While you, I suppose, do as you like?'

'I'll call the tune,' his eyes narrowed on her tear filled,

defiant ones, 'and don't forget it.'

'You expect me to dance to it, regardless of the consequences?'

'What—consequences could there be?'

Her thick lashes dropped. What would his reactions be if she confessed she was falling in love with him? Didn't he guess, being always one step ahead of everyone else, just how involved she was becoming? She kept praying the fierce emotion she felt in her heart was hate, but somehow she doubted it. The sight of Rick's tall, powerful figure in a pair of tight-fitting pants and a shirt which was open to the waist was enough to set her pulses racing. 'Perhaps none,' she attempted to answer his query lightly, 'but a few bruises which will fade.'

'We all collect those,' he said grimly, watching coldly as she turned to leave him. 'Are you finding it difficult to settle in. Ben seems to be doing his best to help.'

'He's the only one who bothers,' she replied flatly.

'What you're suffering from is a dose of self-pity,' he continued indifferently to remove his shirt. 'There are many ways of dealing with that, but only one I'd be inclined to take. If you like I'll spare you an hour or two in the morning and show you a little of the island. A quick tour, if you like, but at least you would be able to find your own way round afterwards.'

So she'd be able to amuse herself and not be a nuisance. Feeling she could almost read his thoughts, she nearly threw his invitation back in his uncaring face, but the thought of his company for even a short time was more than she could resist. Blindly she nodded her head and left him. 'It's probably a good idea,' she agreed, as she closed the door.

The next morning, just as she was beginning to wonder if he had changed his mind, Rick turned up on the front drive in a powerful sports car and took her out. The road followed the coast where the beaches were golden and wide and very beautiful. A lot of the larger properties on the island were situated on its shoreline, with their own private beach, and, despite her former doubts, Emma found she was looking forward to the day immensely.

First she was shown briefly over Rick's own estate, and was amazed at how extensive it was. The house she had already explored although she hadn't gone in any of the bedrooms, apart from her own, or Rick's private study. He didn't offer to show her this, but he did take her over the grounds, then the plantation.

Seeing several men at work, she asked how many he employed.

'Hundreds,' he said briefly, 'during the harvest, but not so many at other times.'

Gazing around the gently rolling acres of green sugar cane, Emma wondered where such large numbers of employees lived, as there didn't seem to be a house in sight.

Patiently Rick explained that a lot of them lived together in their own towns. 'Many of their ancestors were prisoners of war from the '45 rebellion—Scots, who instead of being hanged received the Royal Pardon and were transported to Barbados for life. Some of them eventually came to own their own plantations,' he added. 'Some of them still do.'

Afterwards, as they were both hot, he decided they would find a beach farther north and have a swim before lunch. 'We can leave Bridgetown and the main tourist spots for another day,' he said, after making sure Emma had her bikini.

The water was warm but pleasantly invigorating, yet while Rick was beside her she was too aware of him to really relax. She had known he was well made, but she hadn't realised until she saw him in a pair of brief swimming trunks—which she suspected he only wore for her benefit—just what a perfect physique he had. It would have been much easier, she thought wryly, trying not to stare at him, if he had been old and ugly. At least then he wouldn't have been able to make her feel the way she did.

'Don't ever swim here by yourself,' he instructed curtly, as they waded out of the churning surf.

They had the beach entirely to themselves and she kept her eyes fixed steadily on the lonely reaches of it. 'But you won't always have time to come with me?' She almost added—Or the inclination.

He surprised her by saying, 'Occasionally I might, but when I can't, use the pool in the garden.'

'Ben might bring me,' she retorted, suddenly stung by the indifference in his voice to her defying him.

'I'd rather he didn't,' Rick replied curtly.

'He's very obliging,' she smiled.

'No Ben!' Emma's over-bright smile faded as Rick glanced tautly over her thin body, at the soft golden hair still streaming with water down her slender back, leaving her features as bare and innocent as a newly born babe's. His eyes narrowed, as though he was suddenly seeing her differently and trying to compose a picture which elusively escaped him.

'What if I feel like a little romance?' she asked, driven by what she assessed as a mocking glance to provoke him. She certainly wasn't interested in having a romantic relationship with Ben or any other man, but Rick needn't know that.

A moment later she was regretting her rash question when he drew her swiftly to him and kissed her. During their conversation she had been busy rubbing the water from her face and eyes or she might have seen his arms reaching out. Encircled in them, she realised it was too late to do anything else but submit. The pressure of his mouth increased, and wriggle as she might, she couldn't escape it.

Lifting his head, Rick stared into her dazed eyes, his own darkening. 'I've told you before, you have a very provocative mouth,' he said softly.

She was raising her hands to push him away when a huge wave swept over their lightly clad bodies, the suction of the receding water moulding them together. Her eyes widened and she gasped as she felt his natural response to her thin but very feminine figure. Yet when she tried to pull back the sand was drawn from under her feet, making her cling to him.

Her weight wasn't great, but the sand undermined his balance as well, toppling them both on to the sea bed where the next wave engulfed them completely.

Half drowning in sea water and warm, sensuous feeling, Emma could do nothing as Rick took her mouth again, pinning her body with his to keep her under him on the fine, shifting sand. Wildly she clutched at him, aware only of her reeling senses, while some pagan-like emotion drew them fiercely together. Unconsciously she gasped as he went on kissing her, his mouth hardening with a desire which seemed reflected in the driving force of his limbs.

'Emma?' he muttered against her trembling mouth, 'Emma? Let me love you.'

If he hadn't spoken she couldn't have refused him anything. Why did he ask? she wondered, unable immediately to escape the deep yearning inside her. Why didn't he just take?

When instinctively she said no, without meaning to, he exclaimed harshly, 'You haven't refused other men.'

As the tide receded, he grasped a handful of her streaming hair, breaking the contact of their lips long enough to stare at her. His eyes, she saw dazedly, were full of raw flames. He was aroused and wanting her, but any woman might have done.

'Let me go, Rick.' The words were difficult to get out

past the ones she really wanted to utter. Knowing she loved him and was refusing a chance of belonging to him brought tears to her eyes. Helplessly she felt them streaming down her cheeks, as the weight of his body pressing down between her legs hurt.

He let her go at once, with the air of a man full of contempt. 'I've told you before, you're a little tease,' he rasped, pulling her up beside him.

Unable to reply coherently, Emma stood shaking her head. Noticing her distress, he enquired coldly.

'Did I hurt you?'

'No,' but her voice broke.

'Then why weep?'

'Why does any woman weep?' she did her best to avoid a straight answer.

'Why indeed?' he murmured dryly. 'Usually to help them get their own way. Unfortunately men become hardened to that kind of blackmail, especially with someone like you.'

'Oh, leave me alone,' she muttered, turning from him with a twist of her thin body, to run up the beach. As she got back into her clothes she felt she hated him because he clearly considered her too sophisticated to be genuinely upset. She hated herself, too, for crying over a man who disliked her. Reminding herself of this, she felt oddly grateful that she had had the strength to say no when he had wanted to make love to her. While she loved Rick, she suspected the emotion which occasionally drew them so violently together had little to do with actual loving. It frightened her even to think of it, the passion which could move through them so strongly, because she feared she might not be able to resist it for ever. Rick would take and then discard, leaving her broken and despairing, without giving her another thought.

Lunch, taken in one of the many hotels that dotted the island, was a silent meal. It wasn't until they reached the coffee stage that Emma found the courage to ask Rick a few questions about Barbados, which she felt might be a safer topic than anything else.

Eventually, however, she heard herself asking, 'Would you tell me about St Lusanda? Is your plantation there the same as at Coral Bay?'

'Who told you about St Lusanda?' he startled her by asking sharply. 'I certainly didn't.'

'No.' Emma realised she had almost made a stupid mistake. It had been Blanche who had told her, and that wouldn't please Rick. 'I—I can't remember,' she stammered uneasily. 'Someone must have done . . .'

'You aren't a good liar, are you?' he rejoined softly. 'At a guess it was Blanche.'

Unhappily, Emma nodded, without attempting to deviate again. 'She only said you spent a lot of time there.'

'And she didn't approve?'

'You probably know she didn't,' Emma replied shortly, 'but it was only because she didn't like the idea of you being away from her.'

'But she liked less the prospect of spending weeks there with me?'

Finding it impossible to deny this, Emma gazed at him uncertainly. 'Perhaps she thought it would be lonely.'

'I'm beginning to think I've had a lucky escape,' Rick retorted cynically. 'Of course,' he added, eyeing Emma dryly, 'it's obviously a case of out of the frying pan into the fire. Would the thought of spending a honeymoon with me on a lonely island deter you, my dear Emma?'

While she knew he was deliberately trying to embarrass her, her heart suddenly leapt and the hand that held her cup of coffee shook. How dared he so callously torment her?

'Are you shaking with fear or anticipation?' he jeered cruelly, watching her hot face.

'Why should I be shaking from either?' she glared at

him defiantly. 'The question won't arise . . .'

'Won't it?' he merely grinned derisively.

'Rick,' suddenly discarding discretion completely, Emma leant over the table eagerly, 'can't we talk sensibly? Honeymoons aside, I would like to see your island. When you go, would you take me?'

'No, I don't think so,' coolly his glance travelled over her again. 'Why should I? There's no entertainment on St Lusanda. We should have to amuse ourselves, and you've made it quite clear that you have no intention of amusing yourself with me.'

The implication of what he said couldn't have been plainer. The flush on Emma's cheeks deepened and in an effort to defend herself she exclaimed indiscreetly, 'Haven't you ever taken Veronica Ray there?'

'Yes,' he replied distantly, 'I have.'

No more—or less—but it was enough. Emma lapsed into a bitter silence, her face white. 'She's very beautiful,' she said at last.

'Yes.'

'Do you like her better than me?'

'I know her better than you.' He stood up with an impatient sigh. 'If you're quite finished, Emma, we can go. I have no intention of becoming the target for a full-scale interrogation.'

Three days later he left for Canada where, he told her, he had business interests. This didn't altogether surprise her as already she had learnt that Canada had many links with the island, both business and otherwise. The association with Canada was a lengthy one. As long ago as the eighteenth century Barbados was importing timber from Halifax and Quebec while in return Canada bought molasses and rum. There were Canadian research stations on the island and a lot of Canadians lived here, while many Barbadians went to Canadian universities and eventually made their homes there. Ben had gone to a

Canadian university, but he told Emma if he settled anywhere it might be Australia.

When she asked Rick when he would be home again,
he said briefly that he wasn't sure, and with that she had
to be content. In a way she was relieved to see him go, as
having to be near him each day, yet so distant, was becoming an intolerable strain. Since the day he had taken
her swimming, she had barely seen him except at dinner,
and this was a meal she had come to hate, as almost
always he ignored her. One evening he had dined out,
Gail had hinted not alone, which only added to Emma's
misery. Was he with Veronica? It was more than likely
as she knew Veronica had spoken to him on the telephone late that afternoon.

Trying to hide her despair wasn't easy. If she had
known it was going to be like this she doubted if she would
ever have married him. Not even Hilda or Blanche's worst
behaviour had seemed as hard to endure as the way Rick
treated her.

During the first few days after he had gone, Emma felt
terribly restless. She missed him, missed, strangely enough,
the arrogance of his commanding figure as he went about
the daily affairs of the plantation. For all he seldom spoke
to her more than was absolutely necessary, she felt completely safe when he was around, as no one ever dared
question his authority. Even Rita knew she could only go
so far. During the evenings, if she persisted in making
Emma the target for her vicious digs, Rick usually silenced
his stepmother with a quelling glance, although he
seldom came to Emma's rescue verbally. Without him
Emma felt surprisingly exposed even as she welcomed the
breathing space his absence gave her

Rita and Gail, now that Emma seemed no longer to
pose any great threat to the security they enjoyed at Coral
Bay, tolerated her but were never very friendly. It was
Ben, she thought, who might have saved her sanity after

Rick left without so much as kissing her goodbye. Without Ben's warm, easygoing companionship, she was sure she would never have survived.

The effects of overwork over the past three years, combined with the tensions of the last few weeks, were impossible to throw off immediately, but gradually Emma managed it. To some extent she learnt to relax again. With a surfeit of sea and sand around her, this wasn't too difficult, and being only nineteen might have helped.

Ben took her fishing—at least, he taught her how to handle the boat while he fished. Having always been fond of boats, she applied herself meticulously to learning all about them, and the activity involved bridged the gap between the non-stop work she had been used to and having nothing to do. Very quickly she became proficient, earning Ben's unstinted admiration.

Her swimming improved, too. She had been good at school and under his expert guidance she soon regained all her old skill. As soon as he considered her good enough he took her snorkelling, fitting her out with a mask and flippers, introducing her to the entrancing underwater beauty of the reefs. Always, when she was in the sea, she was reminded of the last time Rick had kissed her. Sometimes she had to force her thoughts away from the memory of his hard sensuous mouth crushing down on hers while the sea pounded wildly over them.

In an attempt to keep such memories at bay and to subdue her treacherous longings, while Ben was busy on the estate she explored the island on her own, spending some time in Bridgetown. Here she found an excellent hairdresser and beautician who was more than willing to carry on the good work begun by his counterpart in Paris. Soon Emma's skin lost every hint of roughness and glowed with a fine, clear radiance. Her hair, too, began to shine with professional care and her own fundamentally good health. Even her figure improved almost beyond anything she might have hoped for. It rounded out, becoming—she tried not to think of Ben's outrageously frank expression, 'amazingly seductive.'

'Rick won't recognise you,' he teased. 'The whole island's talking of the way you've improved.'

'The whole island?' she protested, her delicate brows raised in mild amusement.

'Well, you know me—I tend to exaggerate,' Ben grinned unrepentantly, 'but I'm not laying it on this time, young Emma. When you first came the women were full of catty remarks, prompted by pity. They're still full of bitchiness, but now it's envy. Secretly some of them would give everything they possessed to look as you do now, and to know how you've done it.'

Emma frowned, never having had any ambition to attract this kind of attention. 'I haven't done anything, Ben. I think I've just recovered . . .'

'Recovered from what, for heaven's sake?' Ben asked curiously, as she hesitated.

'Oh, just this and that,' she forced herself to laugh lightly, as though she didn't really know what she was talking about. She might have said, truthfully, from years of hard work and neglect, but this she preferred to forget. Explanations wouldn't only involve herself and wouldn't be worth it.

Ben appeared to have lost the drift of their conversation anyway, as he renewed his obviously enjoyable study of her. His eyes roamed from her gleaming, golden head to her slim waist, before returning to the now near-perfect curves above it. Suddenly, as she turned uneasily from his intent scrutiny, he drew a shaken breath. 'Emma,' he pleaded hoarsely, 'if you ever tire of Rick, marry me.'

'Just like that?' she laughed, refusing to take him seriously, as she pulled her light jacket tightly around her.

'Why not?' he persisted stubbornly. 'You know I wouldn't neglect you as Rick does.'

As this was something she would be foolish to try and deny, she was silent, nursing her unhappiness. The silence went on and she saw the compassion on Ben's face, as well as something of her own hopelessness. 'Perhaps if I'd been as beautiful as Veronica Ray?' she murmured wistfully.

'Veronica and you aren't in the same street,' Ben returned cryptically.

Which, Emma thought wryly, must prove her appearance hadn't improved as much as she imagined.

When Rita told her after lunch, one day, that Veronica had asked them all to another of the small parties she was so fond of giving, Emma was surprised.

'Why me?' she frowned. 'Are you sure I'm included?'

Rita assured her she was. Veronica had said so.

'Perhaps she's heard how the opposition appears to be improving,' Gail put in carelessly, 'and wants to see for herself.'

Rita's critical eyes swept over Emma in faint surprise, but she wasn't given to admiring other women. When Emma had first arrived she had described her as nondescript, and she rarely reversed an opinion. 'Looks aren't everything,' she stated coldly, speaking to her daughter as though Emma wasn't there. 'A man needs someone able to help him socially. I doubt if Rick will remain satisfied with Emma much longer.'

Emma was still smarting from Rita's frank remarks as she attended Veronica's party with Rick's family a few days later. Ben, despite Rita's obvious disapproval, refused to leave Emma's side. He was so attentive she began to feel embarrassed. He might have been setting himself up as her protector. Nor did he seem to be the only man to fancy himself for this position.

Miles Ray, Veronica's younger brother, a very wealthy bachelor in his own right, having inherited a lot of money, seldom took his eyes from her lovely face. 'I can't think how I haven't noticed you before,' he exclaimed, as he managed, with an expertise which reminded Emma oddly of Rick, to inveigle her away from Ben. Ben had frowned when Miles asked her to dance, but without creating a scene there was no way he could refuse to let her go.

Before they had circled the room twice, Miles asked her to have lunch with him next day. 'If you think I'm in a hurry, it's because I don't want anyone to beat me to it,' he explained, quite seriously.

About to refuse politely, Emma paused. Why not? Why shouldn't she lunch with Miles? He was an extremely personable man of thirty and she liked him. He was young and handsome, as were many of the men on the island, and she felt instinctively that Miles and she might have a lot in common. Besides, wouldn't it be wise not to rely on Ben as much as she had been doing? When he had proposed to her she hadn't for a minute taken him seriously. Now she wasn't so sure. Recently she had seen him gazing at her in a way which made her strangely uneasy, and while she didn't imagine he would ever force his attentions on her, she knew she didn't care for him enough to encourage him. She had grown fond of him in a sisterly kind of way, but that was all. Possibly if she went out with Miles occasionally and Ben didn't see quite so much of her he would soon get over his foolish infatuation.

Pleasantly she smiled at Miles and wondered why he caught his breath. 'I'd love to have lunch with you tomorrow,' she said.

Veronica didn't seem to disapprove of her brother's growing friendship with Emma which, considering how much Veronica disliked her, surprised Emma greatly. Each day Miles went to Bridgetown, where he helped run the huge department store. He worked very hard, but he still found time to show Emma over it. She was amazed at its size, the number of departments and the quality of the stock. She had been in before, but only to make a few hurried purchases from the cosmetics department. Now she realised that the store must contain thousands, maybe millions of pounds' worth of highly priced goods.

Rather dazed, she paused to admire a particularly beautiful bracelet locked in a magnificent display case. The bracelet was studded with diamonds and other priceless, sparkling stones. It immediately caught the eye and Emma smiled in wry appreciation.

At once Miles ordered the hovering assistant to get the key for the case and take the bracelet out. After she did he ordered her to wrap it up.

Then, as Emma blinked uncertainly, he rescinded the order. 'No,' he turned to Emma, 'you'd better try it on first. If you don't care for it there are others.'

Emma stared at him, startled and slightly shocked. When she had heard him telling the assistant to get it out of the case she hadn't dreamt he was going to present her with it. She couldn't possibly accept such an expensive gift from any man—unless it was her husband. This brought her thoughts abruptly to Rick. Wasn't he forever insisting she must forget him, that their marriage was over?—a fact which he soon intended to make official. Perhaps if he was to see her getting involved with other men, he would believe she was at last convinced he meant what he said. And to be able to produce certain proof that other men found her desirable might be the only way she might be able to keep what little pride she had left.

CHAPTER SEVEN

YET, as swiftly as the idea of accepting a gift of jewellery from Miles appealed to Emma, she rejected it. It might be one way of impressing Rick, but it wasn't her way. If she was to take the bracelet, under the present circumstances, she would never know a moment's peace. It was how to tell Miles tactfully. As she stood pondering about this, how best to refuse his present without hurting him, Veronica Ray arrived.

Veronica, her sharp eyes flickering from the sparkling bracelet to Emma, cried, 'Now that would suit you, Emma. But surely Rick keeps you well supplied?'

As Emma flushed brightly, Miles sent his sister a murderous glance. 'Why don't you make yourself scarce, Veronica? What you see here is none of your business.'

'I suppose not.' Veronica made no attempt to move on. 'You can't blame me for being interested, though. This makes the one you and Harley gave me for my birthday look like something off a market stall.'

'You have enough, and you're only my sister,' he added stiffly, as if this explained everything.

'And it doesn't matter that Emma merely happens to be another man's wife?' Veronica sneered.

Miles went white. 'If you don't shut up and get out, Veronica, I'll see you out personally,' he threatened. 'Emma and I understand each other.'

'Won't Rick be pleased to hear that!' Veronica crooned, too well used to quarrelling with her brothers to let an exchange such as this disturb her. 'I bet soon you'll be hoping there's going to be a divorce?' she challenged Miles spitefully.

'If Emma feels the same way as I do,' he gripped

Emma's cold hand tightly. 'I love her, but I don't intend going behind anyone's back, least of all Rick Conway's. I'll tell him to his face I want to marry her.'

If this rather startling announcement took the wind from Veronica's sails for a moment, she soon recovered. 'So Emma could be my sister-in-law?'

'If she'll have me.'

'Oh, please!' As pale as Miles, Emma cut in with a protesting gasp. What had started out as a casual invitation to lunch now seemed to have developed into a nightmare. She liked Miles, but that was all. She certainly didn't wish for the kind of complications which usually led to a lot of unkind gossip. Rick, she feared, if this happened, would be furious, if only because she bore his name. He could justifiably accuse her of dragging it through the mud if this little episode were to become common knowledge throughout the island.

'I can't accept the bracelet, Miles. It was a kind thought . . .' she stammered, still not wanting to hurt him, while her grey eyes entreated him wildly.

'Much too public, darling,' Veronica drawled at her brother. 'Put it in your pocket, Miles, until later. I must remember to mention this to Rick.'

'Will you be quiet!' Miles spoke through his teeth, but he did keep hold of the bracelet, as he grabbed Emma's arm to guide her from the store. He didn't look at Veronica again.

In his car he tossed the bracelet brusquely on the ledge between them. 'You may as well have it,' he persisted.

Emma had never felt so embarrassed in her life. 'I can't take it, Miles, you must know that! Not while I'm married to Rick.'

His eyes narrowed. 'That sounds as though you'll not always be married to him.'

'I—oh, I don't know!' Emma was too distracted and miserable to be completely aware of what she was saying.

'Perhaps not, but while I am I don't want to do anything that might hurt him.'

Miles's mouth tightened and it obviously took an effort to refrain from further comment. 'Veronica's crazy. Her arrival was unfortunate, but I meant what I said about wanting to marry you.'

'You know I can't do that either.'

Suddenly his hand was on her rounded chin, turning her face towards him. 'Don't look so unhappy, darling. I believe I understand more than you think. You're sweet and loyal, honest right through, and I love you. If I can't have you I don't want any other girl.'

Why couldn't Rick have trusted her so implicitly? He had been gone six weeks and he had never once made any attempt to get in touch. When he rang Coral House he spoke to Rita or Ben or his overseer. He had enquired after her, Emma believed, but never asked to speak to her. All the same, she found it impossible to even contemplate being unfaithful to him—which must be one of the world's best jokes. How could she be unfaithful to a man who didn't want her?

'I'm sorry, Miles,' her eyes full of tears she turned away. 'You would be wiser to forget me.'

'We'll see,' he replied, then, 'Why not come and have a cup of tea with me before I take you home? You can't refuse me everything.'

It seemed foolish to capitulate, yet if she didn't wouldn't it tend to dramatise the situation in the wrong way? To avoid giving the impression, however, that she was encouraging him, she did say firmly, as they entered the Ray's beautiful drawing room, 'It would be wiser not to see so much of each other, Miles.'

His eyes darkened bitterly, before he shrugged and smiled. 'Just as you like, but I've promised to go to the party Rita's giving at the end of the week, so I'll have to see you there. After that, we'll see. Why not leave it? You might suddenly discover you care for me more than that handsome husband of yours.'

Emma returned his smile and sighed, but was prevented from replying when Veronica joined them, regardless of her brother's icy glance. Veronica looked in a remarkably good mood, considering the one she had been in when they had left her. For the next half hour she was a model hostess. But just as they were leaving, when Miles was called to the telephone, Emma said she would go and sit in the car, rather than wait in the house. She didn't care, all of a sudden, for the way Veronica was looking at her. She reminded Emma of a cat that had just caught a mouse and was preparing to play with it.

At the end of the week, in an attempt to cheer herself up, Emma dressed more carefully than usual. That afternoon she had gone to Bridgetown and had her hair done and indulged in a facial. She was, in fact, beginning to feel guilty about the number of expensive treatments she had been having as she had no money of her own and had to ask for the bills to be sent to Rick. This was no problem, as far as the salon was concerned, but she couldn't help wondering if Rick would approve, or if it was worth it. While her glowing skin might be beautiful to look at, improved almost beyond recognition, she feared her own pleasure in her new appearance would count for nothing if Rick didn't like it.

In one of her glittering Paris gowns, Emma knew, despite her doubts, that she looked good. Her Paris model might be a little elaborate for a simple party, but she had nothing else. She had purchased several simple day dresses since coming to Barbados, but hadn't wanted to enlarge her wardrobe more than was necessary. Apart from some camisole tops to go with her long skirts, she hadn't bothered with anything else. If her skirts hadn't been in need of pressing, a fact which she had only just discovered, she might have worn one of them this evening.

Ben and Miles were both there when she went downstairs. Both, as she danced with them, assured her she was the most beautiful girl there. So did several of the younger set, with whom Emma was fast becoming popular. The young men especially were beginning to take notice of her a lot. They seemed to like dancing with her and sometimes she caught their eyes wandering to her now very curvaceous figure.

'You're slim yet so sexy, honey,' the more daring of them teased frankly, as though they enjoyed seeing her blush. They were friendly, but they kept their distance. Of this she was glad, but she wondered if some of them would have been so scrupulous if it hadn't been for Rick. Rick, she had soon learnt, commanded a healthy respect on the island among both young and old.

Sometimes Emma, when considering her new popularity, would feel surprised at the shortness of people's memories. When she had first arrived almost everyone had ignored her. Now it was different, but while she responded happily to the new friendship she was offered she wasn't sure that she would ever fit in. She definitely wouldn't with the more uninhibited set, she thought, looking around. She much preferred those who, like herself, favoured a quieter way of life. If she had been able to continue as Rick's wife, this would have suited her fine—the odd evening out, perhaps dining and dancing, after helping him at home, or wherever he might be. What she would really enjoy, she mused, allowing her thoughts to run on, was sailing with him. She imagined, when it came to snorkelling, he would be able to show her an underwater world which few might know about. They might have gone riding together, too, in the early mornings, and listened to records or just talked before going to bed. Farther than the top of the stairs with him she never allowed herself to go. Deliberately she refrained from speculating on Rick as a lover. It made her heart race wildly to even consider a bedroom door closed against the world and Rick taking her in his arms.

'You're miles away!' Ben gave her a cross little shake as they danced, his eyes sulky yet curious.

She came to with a strangled breath. 'I'm sorry,' she flushed awkwardly. 'Yes, I'm afraid I was.'

'Who was the lucky fellow?'

'Who . . .?' Blankly she stared up at him. 'Oh, I see . . .'

'Don't begin to deny it, he said dryly, considering her deepening colour. 'For all Rick neglects you, I do believe you still dream of him!'

'A girl has to dream of someone,' she tried to sidetrack him by being flippant.

'Try me,' Ben's arms tightened. 'I love you, baby.'

Emma smiled, shaking her head at him, but was relieved when the dance finished. Ben was getting too intense. Two nights ago he had begged for a goodnight kiss. If Rita knew she would be furious, as she had a girl already chosen for him, the only child of wealthy parents. When someone put on another disc he was reluctant to relinquish Emma to Miles.

'You don't want to dance with him,' he muttered insultingly, not using Miles's name.

Miles's fair skin flushed, but he tried to treat it as a joke. 'I hope I'm as good as you, Ben,' he exclaimed.

Anxiously Emma put her hand on Miles's arm, drawing him away. She became aware of Veronica's silent regard, of the spite in her eyes. What was she whispering to Rita about? Why were they both staring at her so contemptuously?

She was so disturbed, she was grateful, after a few minutes, when Miles suggested a stroll in the garden. 'I feel a bit off,' he said. 'Would you mind?'

'No.' She glanced at him, concerned. 'You should have mentioned it before. Can't I get you something?'

'No,' he refused grimly, 'a breath of fresh air will do the trick, and a chance to talk to you.'

They had left the terrace to traverse one of the wide paths. 'Talk to me?' She hadn't seen him since the afternoon when she had had tea with him and Veronica. She had refused to go out with him again. It probably wasn't sensible to be out here with him, but he did look strained and ill. And it was near the house. She didn't think Miles would ever force his attentions on any girl without encouragement, but perhaps, she thought regretfully, that was what she had been giving him, by going out with him, even the few times she had.

Unhappily she sighed. It was only friendship she had been after. She hadn't dreamt she would be able to really attract a man, but if Ben and Miles hadn't been seriously attracted would they have offered marriage? Of course such an offer could have been made to cover more devious intentions—while because of Rick they felt safe that she couldn't accept. On the other hand, if they'd merely had seduction in mind would they have begged her to get a divorce?

'What is it you want to talk about?' she asked abruptly, for the second time that evening not caring to continue with her own thoughts.

'You,' he said doggedly, pausing on the path. 'You and your marriage, I suppose.'

'It's . . .' she hesitated, colouring painfully as she took a deep breath. 'That's something I don't want to talk about, Miles. It only involves Rick and me, and I think I asked you the other day to leave me alone.'

'So now it's none of my business,' he muttered between his teeth. 'Oh, Emma,' his voice roughened hoarsely, 'you must know damn well I love you, and I believe you've given me reason to think you care for me.' His eyes darkened with pain as he gazed at her. 'I don't forget for a moment that you're married. Do you think I could?

Isn't it always in front of me, tormenting me? Torturing me would be nearer the mark! How can a man forget something that hurts like a knife in his side? My only comfort is that yours is not a normal marriage. Veronica has told me Rick more or less admits it.'

'Miles, please!' Who was he to talk of torture? Emma was white and stricken that Rick had chosen to discuss their affairs like this. He might be able to, but she couldn't bring herself to talk about their marriage with anyone. To continue in silence might be almost unendurable, but it was the only way. Not for her the relief that Rick obviously obtained from talking over his marital problems with his latest girl-friend.

'Emma!' Miles refused to take any notice of her distress, believing he knew the cause of it. He was so rapidly losing control that her alarm grew and showed in the helpless widening of her eyes as he raced on. 'Emma, I want you—but for my wife. Get a divorce—God knows it's easy enough these days. I love you. I want to marry you, to be able to look after you for the rest of your life.'

Dear heavens, were all the men on the island going mad? No—Emma tried firmly to calm down. It was only Ben and Miles who persisted in going to such foolish lengths. It must be another of fate's cruel jokes that Ben happened to be Rick's stepbrother while Miles was Veronica's family. Rick would be furious if anything of this ever reached his ears. Emma shivered. What a perfect fool she had been!

'Say something, Emma, please!' His voice thickening, Miles grasped her stiff shoulders. 'You must have guessed how I felt. I wasn't sure how you did, not until you accepted my bracelet.'

'Let go of her Ray!'

Horrified, Emma twisted in Miles's grasp. Ben stood over them, his face white with temper. 'She belongs to me!' he shouted at Miles, despite Emma's efforts to silence him. 'You'd better get out of here!'

Miles retaliated grimly, although he obviously had no ambition to create a scene. 'Don't be a fool, Ben,' he snapped. 'Use your sense. You couldn't hope to give her what I can, and I don't believe she even cares for you.'

For Emma it was like a nightmare after that. Ben, faced with indisputable facts, sought to relieve his frustration in the best way he knew. Instinctively, as rage overwhelmed his common sense, he lashed out. Emma, terrified something like this was going to happen, tried to come between the two men, but received the glancing impact of Ben's fist on the side of her face.

Ben, amazingly, didn't appear to hear her cry of pain, or if he did it failed to penetrate the mounting violence of his emotions. He had always disliked Miles Ray and this opportunity to avenge himself of past slights, if nothing else, seemed too good to miss. Blindly he thrust Emma aside, so she fell against a thorny bush, doing more damage to her already bruised features.

Dazed, Emma opened her eyes to stare, in a kind of fascinated horror, at the ensuing fight. Miles and Ben were evenly matched, although Ben was the younger and heavier. Miles might have more of the world's wealth, but it became apparent that Ben was superior in strength. His fist hit Miles squarely and he went down with a thump.

Not so easily defeated, he shot up again and battled on, while Emma, scrambling hysterically to her own two feet, tried in vain to part them. She never knew whose elbow caught her as she attempted to stop the fight, but, half fainting from a blow which made her feel sick, she toppled over, tears of helpless mortification running down her face. Huddled in a heap, she heard the fight continuing, feeling so weak that she wasn't even able to run and seek help.

Then suddenly, from the darkness, completely unexpected, another man appeared, one taller and broader, with lean, well disciplined muscles of steel. Within seconds he had sized up the situation and torn the two other men apart. He shook them like rats, while the language he used was far from refined. In the light from the rising moon, his face was illuminated with an anger that far surpassed that of either of the men he was holding.

Terrified, Emma shrank back, covering her sore, tear-drenched face with her hands as she tried to pretend Rick wasn't there. In vain she hoped he didn't know she was. Surely he didn't? Otherwise he couldn't possibly be uttering such terrible things, none of which were designed for the ears of a lady!

It soon became obvious he did know she was there, as he turned on her almost immediately, his voice still full of barely controlled fury. 'What the hell do you think you've been playing at, Emma? The minute my back's turned . . .'

He had been gone nearly seven weeks! Emma would have liked to have accused him, but was too choked with sobs and shock to be able to manage even a single word in her own defence.

'Look here, Conway, let me explain.' Miles's face was bright red as he strove to recover both his dignity and breath.

'Shut up!' Rick snarled, turning his back to him.

Ben gasped and spluttered, staring with hatred at Miles. Miles could hit hard, but he was certain he would have been the winner. If Rick hadn't interfered. Swiftly he transferred his sullen indignation to his stepbrother.

'He thinks he owns Emma,' he snapped, 'just because she's been going out with him.'

Rick, as if suddenly finding the distraught, huddled figure of his wife particularly deplorable, ordered her grimly back to the house. 'Get out of my sight—and stay there!'

Emma couldn't look at him, she felt too apprehensive at what she might see in his face to try. She would like to have said something on behalf of Miles and Ben, but her bewilderment at what had happened was so great it left her mind a complete blank. All she could think of was Rick's hate. After this he would surely hate her more than ever, and she felt lacerated more by this than by the pain of the blows she had received.

Upstairs, in her room, she crouched on her bed as though the strength of Rick's wrath had already fallen on her. Clumsily she managed to dispose of her dress and huddle into the old woollen dressing-gown she had brought from the farm in England. It was the one thing she hadn't liked to leave home without, and now she felt oddly comforted by its familiar warmth. The semi-tropical night was warm, but she shivered with fear, which affected her like cold.

When Rick arrived she was still in a huddle. Her face was a mess from Ben's accidental blows and tears, so she kept it hidden against her pillows. Feverishly she hoped that Rick's anger might have abated, but she judged from the sound of his voice as he spoke that it had not.

'I can't leave you five minutes,' he said harshly, 'and you revert to what you were before I married you.'

'What was that?' she whispered.

'A slut!' he exclaimed emphatically.

Shrinking away from his contempt, Emma sobbed afresh. 'It wasn't my fault, what you saw,' she gulped incoherently.

'Whose fault was it, then?' She could feel his glance piercing the back of her head. 'You must have led them on and then said something to set them against each other!'

'I haven't encouraged either of them.' She knew suddenly she could say this quite honestly. 'I don't know what they expected from me. They had a lot of silly ideas . . .'

'About what?' he prompted sharply, as her voice trailed off.

'Oh, nothing.' She couldn't bring herself to mention how both Ben and Miles had asked her to marry them. Quite probably by now they had both changed their minds. Anyway, Rick would never believe their intentions had been honourable.

She knew she was right when Rick snarled, 'Men don't fight over a woman for nothing, and from you they could only look for one thing. As you've neither beauty or breeding it couldn't be anything else.'

Desperately hurt, she tried to stifle anguished sobs. 'You're being completely unfair!'

'Unfair!' he exploded on a tightening breath. 'Don't you realise I might have done murder tonight, if someone hadn't warned me what you were up to in time?'

'Someone warned you?' Emma heard herself asking in bewilderment.

'Someone kindly told me you'd accepted a valuable piece of jewellery from Miles Ray.'

'But I didn't!' alarm made Emma's voice hoarse, 'He—I admit he wanted to give me something. He even brought it with him to the car, but I still refused.'

'I don't want to hear any more lies!' She heard Rick's teeth snap and the sharp twist of his body as he grasped the handle of one of her dressing table drawers, pulling it open. As she removed her hands from her horrified eyes, she saw him lift out Miles's bracelet. 'As you've been showing it off to other people, why not me?' Rick rasped. 'What am I to suppose this is?'

Completely stunned, Emma stared at it, unconscious now of her bruised and blotched face. The last time she had seen the bracelet it had been still in Miles's car. He had stopped insisting she should have it, as he eventually came to understand her point of view, and had left it in the car when they had gone into his house for tea. Afterwards, when he had driven her home, it had gone, but she hadn't mentioned it. She had concluded, she recalled, that he had remembered and collected it and locked it away, when he had gone to the kitchen to order their tea.

Someone must have put it in her drawer, but who? Blankly she continued staring at the sparkling stones in Rick's hand. 'I—I just don't know what to say,' she stammered. 'I haven't any idea how it got there, and that's the truth.'

'Would you know the meaning of the word?' he asked insultingly, thrusting the bracelet in his pocket as he came to jerk her ruthlessly upright on the bed. He was so close his breath seemed to scorch her bruised skin and she closed her eyes against the picture he must be seeing. All her newly acquired beauty had gone, and her figure, wrapped in the old shapeless dressing-gown, must be exactly as he remembered it.

Because she could feel tremors running through her from where his hands gripped, she swallowed, saying less than convincingly, 'If I'd taken the stupid thing why wasn't I wearing it tonight? Wouldn't you have expected a girl of my disreputable character to be showing it off?'

'You might have been.'

'Why don't you check?'

'Be quiet!' His voice was icy cold and his fingers bit deeper. 'I've had just about enough of your lies and deceit. Your family have a rare gift for it. And you—you've caused nothing but trouble since I first met you, and it seems you aren't satisfied yet.'

'You despised me, but it didn't stop you from using me,' she retorted.

'If you served a purpose I'm certainly paying for it,' he exclaimed, his eyes grimly examining her hurt face. 'Now, on top of everything else, I find I'll have to take you to St Lusanda, otherwise everyone will imagine I've been beating you up.'

'It was Ben and Miles,' tears overflowed again and she

sniffed hastily, 'but it wasn't their fault I got in the way.'

'And how would I explain that, exactly?' Rick's voice was loaded with sarcasm, his eyes scornful. 'Do I say— You must excuse my wife Her two lovers happened to be fighting over her?'

'No!' Emma's flush did nothing to improve her appearance. 'They weren't—aren't . . .'

'Then stop arguing,' he cut her off tersely. 'You'll go to St Lusanda and stay there until I allow you to return. A few weeks on the island with only myself for company might straighten you out, if nothing else does. If I feel like it I might even teach you a lesson you won't forget in a hurry!'

If Rick had loved her and asked her to go to St Lusanda with him Emma would have been delighted. Now such a prospect held little joy. She was terrified that, alone together on the island, she might betray how much she had come to love him, while he felt nothing for her but hate.

'I'd rather go back to England,' she begged huskily, as he continued to study her face.

His eyes, moving darkly over her, narrowed. 'If you did people would only believe the same as they would here. And I have no wish to supply Blanche, yet, with such irrefutable proof of my broken marriage.'

Emma flinched, repeating miserably, 'I've told you it was Ben and Miles . . .'

'And they'll pay for it,' he assured her, between his teeth, his eyes of a sudden glittering diabolically. 'You can take it from me they'll suffer, much more than you're doing.'

'Rick,' she gasped, 'you—you won't do anything foolish? I'm—I'm not worth it,' she added, fearful that he might be letting himself in for a lot of trouble and thinking that might deter him.

'I realise,' he replied grimly, 'but I can look after myself—as well as other people. I'll get Belasco to take you to St Lusanda in the morning. I'll follow later.'

He sounded so adamant Emma huddled deeper in the old worn robe. 'Please, Rick, don't make me go,' she protested weakly. 'I promise I haven't done anything to justify being sent away like this.'

'That's not the story I've heard,' he snapped, as if her insistence infuriated him. 'You've been behaving shamelessly. Dogs don't fight over a bone that isn't available.'

'I won't go,' she cried, while dully realising the futility of protesting further. Rick would never believe she was innocent. Perhaps it suited him to think her guilty of the worst possible things?

'You'll go!' For a moment his eyes smouldered fiercely and to her dismay he suddenly pulled her to him, holding her powerless as his mouth descended to silence her protesting cry.

As his mouth brutally crushed hers, she hated him, but as she slumped against him and took fire she was again reminded that the state of her mind bore little relation to the reactions of her traitorous body.

His kiss was harsh but brief, but before he lifted his head he muttered darkly against her shaking lips, 'Every woman I've taken to the island, so far, has hated it. The isolation upsets them and they're glad to return to what they call civilisation. For you there won't be any such chance, but I promise not to deprive you for ever of that which you obviously can't do without.'

Belasco took her to the island next morning in Rick's powerful motor launch. It was fitted out with special seats and harness and Belasco told her proudly that the boss used it when he went fishing for barracuda. The powerful diesel engines cut through the water, soon leaving Barbados behind. At first Emma wondered that Rick dared entrust such an expensive boat to anyone else but himself. When she was younger, however, she had done a lot of sailing with her father and his friends and she soon saw that Belasco was an expert. There was nothing for her to worry about and, not knowing whether this was good or bad, she settled down against the bulkhead, alone with her thoughts.

Last night, after issuing what seemed very like a savage threat, Rick had left her. A few minutes later he returned with hot milk and brandy, standing over her until she drank every drop. Before leaving her this time he had told her to lock the door behind him and not to open it to anyone. She had been too nervous to do anything else but obey, but she had been relieved that no one had even tried to see her. After bathing her face and using the ointment he brought her, she had gone to bed and tried to sleep.

Rick hadn't been around this morning. It had been Belasco who had knocked and asked gently if she was ready to leave. In the early morning, before the other servants had been up, they had slipped away unseen. Had Rick been watching from some hidden vantage point? Emma was so sure he must have been that she had gone with Belasco quietly, refusing to give Rick the undoubted satisfaction of an undignified struggle.

Now, as she gazed across the blue waters of the Caribbean, she wondered what lay in store for her. No matter how she tried she couldn't forget the hard fury on Rick's face when he had talked to her the previous evening. What did he intend doing? He might not intend carrying out his veiled threats. He might only mean to keep her on St Lusanda until it was time to get rid of her altogether. Wearily she closed sore eyes against the growing dazzle of the sun. She had longed to see his island, but not in this way! Occasionally, throughout the morning, she was aware of Belasco gazing at her curiously and she hoped, with a kind of morbid amusement, that he didn't imagine Rick was responsible for the state of her face.

'I bumped into a tree in the garden,' she at last said uncomfortably. She hadn't meant to offer any explanation, but a tree had been part of it, and that might satisfy him.

'Yes, miss,' he returned, so poker-faced she was sure he doubted her story. 'Sure looks nasty.'

'My husband,' she stressed the latter word as Belasco had called her 'miss', and while she felt she must be mistaken, his tones seemed to question she was properly married. 'My husband,' she repeated severely, 'gave me something to put on it, so it will soon be all right.'

'Everything soon be all right,' Belasco said earnestly, suddenly nodding his dark head.

Emma merely shrugged, turning away, unable, just then, to care whether it would be or not.

St Lusanda was certainly different from Barbados. Emma saw this immediately. She had lost count of the hours it took to get there. Part of the way she dozed, tired from her almost sleepless night and the drama which had led up to it. At other times she had drunk the coffee Belasco kept her endlessly supplied with and stared sightlessly out to sea, trying hopelessly to visualise the future— the endless, empty stretches of it.

The island was larger than she had thought it would be. Belasco appeared to confirm this when he told her that a lot of people lived there, many of whom went about their own business when they weren't engaged on the sugar plantations. They anchored by a jetty set in a beautiful greeny-blue lagoon and the few islanders who were gathered there glanced at her without too much curiosity. As she regarded them, Emma was very conscious of her discoloured face. She had done her best with a heavy make-up, but she had nothing that would completely disguise the ravages of her recent ordeal.

None of the islanders seemed to realise she was Rick Conway's new wife, and Belasco didn't tell them. Emma

was grateful to him for preserving her anonymity even
while she was aware they would soon discover who she
was. On an island this size it would be impossible to keep
such a secret for ever.

A driver was there for them as they came in. Again
Belasco handled her gently as he helped her from the boat
to the jetty and then to the waiting truck. He took particular care to see she was comfortable before he sat himself protectively beside her and instructed the driver to
move off.

The road was rough but by no means unbearably so
and the island was so beautiful Emma didn't think she
would have noticed if it had been. St Lusanda appeared
to be encircled by pale silvery sands and blue seas which
lapped coves which in turn were sheltered by the green
mountains behind them. Over all lay a perfect peace, but
she also sensed something of the isolation Rick had hinted
at. Yet it wasn't this, so much, that made her suppress a
sudden shiver. It was the frightening premonition that
when she left she would be a vastly different girl from the
one she was now.

CHAPTER EIGHT

As they reached the house it soon became obvious what
Rick meant when he talked of it as not being too popular
with his lady-friends. The house, though large and solidly
built, had none of the elegant lines of his home on
Barbados. Inside the accommodation was spacious enough
and clean and well cared for, but Emma couldn't imagine
either Veronica or Blanche liking it.

Upstairs there were four large bedrooms, all containing
massive pieces of dark old furniture. She saw at once
which one belonged to Rick. It was as tidy as the others,
but a pile of paperbacks lay on the bedside table and
when she looked the drawers of an old polished chest contained several of his shirts. Having made sure of this, she
chose for herself the room farthest away from it. Apart
from Rick's, the others were more or less the same, so she
didn't think he would mind which one she occupied.
Belasco had told her that a married couple with daughters
lived at the rear of the house and looked after everything,
as well as the boss when he was here. Dinner would be
ready in an hour, which gave her plenty of time to unpack
and get settled in.

The housekeeper was called Josephine. She said she was
of French extraction, and sent her daughter, a pleasant
girl, to unpack for Emma. This left Emma with nothing
to do but shower and change. Despite this, she was too
exhausted after dinner to do anything else but take another shower and crawl into bed. When Josephine fussed
with hot coffee and brandy, Emma did her best to assure
her there was nothing wrong, that she was only a little
tired and would be quite recovered by morning.

When Josephine had gone, still with a worried frown

on her face, Emma lay for quite a while staring up at
the ceiling, wondering what Rita and Gail would make of
her sudden disappearance. She had seen nothing of them
since Rick arrived and was curious as to how he would
explain her somewhat precipitate departure from
Barbados. While she tried to stop them, her thoughts kept
returning to the mysterious appearance of Miles's bracelet
in her drawer. How could it have got there? Somehow
she found it difficult to believe Miles had been responsible,
but obviously it could only have been him. He must have
been determined that she should have it, she decided
bitterly, and because of the devious way he had gone
about it she had little hope of ever persuading Rick that
she hadn't accepted it willingly.

Awakening next morning from a restless, dream-torn
sleep, Emma was glad to leave her bed and dress. Hastily
she found a pair of shorts and a matching top and, after
completing a brief toilet, saw that her appearance wasn't
quite as ruined as she had feared.

Her face was still bruised, but the bruises weren't as
noticeable as they had been yesterday, and the rest of her,
apart from her face, was no different. Her figure remained
greatly improved from when Rick had last seen her. It
had been the way in which he had looked at her, after
their quarrel in the bedroom at Coral House, which had
mentally transformed her back to a plain young girl.
Perhaps for him she would never be any different. While
there might be rose-tinted spectacles, there might also be
darkly tinted ones, through which a man might never see
over clearly.

Time on the island, Emma found, passed gently. With
no immediate worries, she spent her days idly. True, her
thoughts continued to torment her, but on the whole she
felt more relaxed. Josephine and her family looked after
her so well she hadn't anything else to do but amuse herself. This she did by exploring the island, or just swimming

and lying on the hot sand while, at a discreet distance, Belasco and another man guarded over her constantly.

Once, knowing how much all the family relied on him, she asked Belasco how they would be managing without him on Barbados. He had merely laughed and shrugged his great shoulders and said he had no idea.

'Won't do them any real harm, Miss Emma,' he grinned. 'Maybe the ladies will appreciate me more when I return there. But that I can't do until the boss arrives.'

While at first Emma had feared Rick's immediate arrival, it was in fact almost a week before he turned up. She had begun to think he might not come at all, that he meant to confine her to a solitary imprisonment on the beautiful island. And while she felt this would present no great punishment, her heart hungered strangely for even a glimpse of him. When he did arrive it was so unexpected, he took her completely by surprise. He walked in one evening just before dinner, to catch her as she was returning late from the beach.

Half way up the stairs, where he was obviously going in search of her, he paused to glance back at her with cool indifference. Then he frowned as his eyes became fixed. Emma, having entered the house by the kitchen quarters and left Belasco chatting to Josephine's husband, was stunned. The colour left her face, which she knew would show up the now almost faded bruising. Her heart beating rapidly, she fought for composure as her eyes widened on Rick's tall, dominant figure.

As he turned slowly to retrace his steps, she wished he would stop staring at her. His eyes were mere slits and he appeared to be inspecting her inch by inch, going carefully over the new silky smoothness of her skin, the soft, seductive curves of her slender young body.

Shrinking under such a closely calculating surveillance, she wasn't sure what to expect, and surprise shot through her when he commented quite casually, 'I see you've settled in.'

'Yes,' she tried to adopt the coolness of his tones but failed. 'Yes,' she repeated, attempting to make her voice stronger.

When he nodded but appeared to have nothing further to say, she enquired nervously, 'How did you get here?'

'By boat,' he replied. 'I have more than one and did a little fishing on the way.'

'I see . . .' so he hadn't been in any hurry?

As if losing interest, Rick turned from her abruptly, his jaw hard. 'I want to shower before I eat. Are you coming upstairs?'

'I suppose so.' She trailed behind him apprehensively. 'Now that you're here, I suppose you'll expect me to change for dinner?'

'I like to keep up certain standards,' he agreed smoothly, 'but we don't have to be as formal as we are on Barbados.'

'I—I wasn't sure if you would bother,' she faltered, wondering with amazement how she came to be going on at such lengths about something so trivial when she had far more serious things on her mind. Uneasily she blamed Rick. He unnerved her with his fixed, cynical stare—what was there about her which held his attention so keenly? He kept looking back at her, as she reluctantly followed him, as if he couldn't help himself. She noted, though, that he didn't appear to like what he saw.

'I bother,' he returned briefly, 'even if it's just a clean shirt. It shouldn't be impossible for you to find a short dress.' Again his glance flicked her long, slim legs which her brief shorts left bare.

Why did he taunt and mock so? 'I've been on the beach,' she said, seeking irrationally to excuse herself. If she didn't get away from him soon, she would probably find herself apologising for even being here! For even daring to exist.

Rick merely nodded as he halted outside his bedroom door, holding it open. When, head bent, Emma tried to walk past him, he grabbed her arm. 'Where do you think you're going?'

'To my room.' She found it impossible to look at him, to meet the cynicism which she knew would be in his eyes. 'You don't have any communicating rooms here,' she hastened, 'so I chose the one over there. It's very pleasant . . .'

'And I'm not?'

Something in his voice which she failed to understand made her go stiff all over. 'I—I wasn't talking about you,' she protested.

'Weren't you?' he jeered. 'Well, this is my room, so it follows it's yours, too.'

Emma tried not to clench her fingers, not wishing him to guess her growing agitation. 'We—we didn't share at Coral House!'

'No,' his hard mouth curled at the way her voice wobbled. 'That was because I was giving you time to get used to me, to being married. Unfortunately charitable gestures are rarely repaid. Some other man beat me to it.'

'Just what are you trying to say, Rick?' Emma, although she was trembling, knew a sudden urgency to know what he was talking about.

'I mean,' his eyes glinted harshly on her dazed, bewildered ones, '—if you must have it spelt out, that I'm no fool. I felt the way you responded, when I held you in my arms after the fiasco in the gardens. I suppose you merely closed your eyes and imagined I was Ray or Ben, but I could tell by your kisses someone had taught you a lot. And that's not the only change I perceive,' he added insolently, his dark blue eyes smouldering with anger as they swept over her.

Half aware of what he was hinting at, she felt a tearful rage catch her heart. 'If you must know,' she burst out impulsively, 'you're the only man I've ever kissed.'

For her pains, his head went back on his strong neck and he laughed. There wasn't much mirth to his laughter, but it hurt all the same, hurt and humiliated! 'God!' he rapped, his eyes suddenly black with anger, 'if you tell me any more of your impossible little stories I won't be responsible for what I might do.'

There seemed no logic in the argument they were having, no way she could reason with him. He just wouldn't believe anything she said. Hopelessly she hung her bright head. 'Let me stay in the other room, Rick,' she pleaded. 'How can we share a room when you hate me so much?'

Ignoring this, he commanded abruptly, 'Get your things. We'll start as we should have done when we were first married. After all,' his smile was even harsher than his laughter had been, 'why shouldn't we enjoy each other while we're together? We might have had an unusual honeymoon, but there's no reason now why we shouldn't live like a normal couple. Until we part, that is.'

Feeling slightly sick, Emma stared at him. He sounded so reasonable, if it wasn't for what he was suggesting! Her eyes widened apprehensively. She didn't know why she should suddenly suspect he was secretly seething with an anger more terrible than anything she had known before. Something about him made her tremble with a peculiar kind of terror and give in to him weakly.

'I'll get dressed and then pack everything.'

When Rick nodded grimly and let go of her arm, she clutched the spot where his fingers had dug deeply and fled.

Feverishly, in her room, she showered, scarcely realising what she was doing. After drying herself she hastily put on the first dress she came to, a simple little cotton. Rick would insist she went down for dinner, but what sort of meal would it be with such an atmosphere of distrust between them? And afterwards? She could only hope Rick would come to his senses before he did something he might always regret. Perhaps, she prayed silently, he would change his mind about the rooms if she didn't do anything else to antagonise him.

After hearing his bedroom door open and no other sound for several minutes, she believed he must have gone down without her. She was about to slip thankfully from her own room when he walked in.

Ignoring, as before, her look of dismay, he said, 'I'll give you a hand with your things. You seem quite recovered from your overdose of popularity, but you can't afford to take risks. You still look frail.'

How hateful he could be! How was it possible for a man to sound so caring yet taunting? 'I haven't had time to pack,' Emma stammered.

Rick laughed, his eyes glinting. 'You're only going across the passage, not to the other side of the world. You weren't thinking of packing properly, were you? I can easily carry everything.'

He sounded so cool and sensible, while Emma didn't feel either. Yet when he carefully gathered all her clothes together in his arms, she found herself without the courage to protest. He even, she saw, as she hovered behind him pale-faced, put everything neatly away in two of his empty drawers, hanging her few long dresses next to his suits in the spacious wardrobe.

'There,' he murmured softly, as though he were talking to a fretful child, 'nothing to it, as you can see. We'll be nice and cosy in here, just the two of us.'

Did he really believe that? Did he actually mean her to sleep in that huge, old-fashioned bed with him? Colour flooded her pale cheeks and she swallowed painfully. 'Rick—you know this wasn't part of our—er—bargain . . .'

'Neither was Ray,' he shrugged, with deceptive mildness. 'It was you who first broke the agreement between us when you attempted to drag my name through the—shall we say—dust of Barbados. In view of that, why should I bother to stick to rules?'

Emma hated the derision she saw in his face. How unfair he was! What about his own relationship with Veronica Ray? Didn't he ever think about that? She was willing to bet his friendship with Veronica was no way near as innocent as that which she had shared with Ben or Veronica's brother!

Unhappily she sighed, meeting Rick's coldly belligerent stare. To argue with him now, she realised, would be futile, and she was grateful when she heard the gong. There was a great brass gong in the hall which Belasco declared was enough to waken the restless souls of his ancestors. The noise of it penetrated loudly upstairs, and she used it as an excuse for not replying to Rick's last taunt.

While dinner was being served he studied her curiously across the table. Feeling the anger still smouldering within him, Emma wondered uneasily if her supposedly regrettable behaviour had really dealt such a blow to his pride. If it had, it could surely only have been a very small one—nothing, surely, to justify such icy, disapproving eyes and tightening lips. Fearing, as the glint in his eyes deepened, that he was about to reopen the subject, she interposed swiftly,

'You haven't told me how you got on in Canada.'

'As well as usual,' he replied suavely, as the servant withdrew and they started on the first course. Emma noticed wryly how everything on the table sparkled, how extra care had been taken because the boss was here. The shrimp cocktail they were eating was delicious and as an entrée made a nice change from the usual piece of egg on a lettuce leaf which she was given.

Rick said nothing more and she wished he would talk

to her about Canada, if he didn't want to discuss his business there. Or did he think that because her stay in his life was to be so brief, it wasn't worth talking to her about anything? 'You never wrote, or rang me,' she said, tears stinging her eyes along with a real sense of grievance.

'Did you expect me to?' he snapped.

'No,' she hesitated, as he rang for the next course, 'but I thought you might. It——' she swallowed, 'it made me feel lonely when you didn't.'

'And when your loneliness grew intolerable, you consoled yourself with other men.'

Helplessly she frowned. That hadn't been what she meant. 'I—I went out with Ben occasionally, yes, I'll admit. He taught me things . . .'

Rick's eyes slitted to steel splinters. 'He won't again. He's off to Australia.'

'Not—not because of me, I hope?' Among other things, if Rick had blamed her, Emma shivered to imagine Rita's wrath.

'It was the sensible course to take. He was going soon, in any case.'

'But not just yet.'

'Does it make any difference?'

Hating the jeering note in his voice, she exclaimed, 'It might, to Ben. If his sudden departure was based on the wrong motives.'

'I think not,' Rick returned harshly, draining his glass which he immediately replenished.

Painfully, Emma watched him. 'The relationship between the two of you has always been a good one. He practically worships you. I would hate to think I'd been responsible for any trouble, but I . . .'

'Forget it,' he cut in brusquely. 'Everything's been taken care of.'

'And Miles?' she whispered, suddenly frightened and

made reckless by such ruthlessness. 'How did you deal with him?'

'Ah, now I detect real concern!' A cruel smile tugged at the corners of his mouth. 'Miles is too besotted to do anything but protest your innocence, but, like you, is unfortunately lacking in proof.'

'You surely didn't accuse him of anything?' she asked hollowly.

'I didn't stop long enough for that,' he rejoined curtly. 'I merely returned his bracelet and told him exactly what I thought of him.'

Imagining what that would be, Emma shivered. The pleasure Rick had derived was still written clearly on his face. Suddenly desperate to change the subject, she looked down at her plate. 'Did you stay in Canada all the time you were away?'

'No.'

'So that's all you're going to tell me?' Glancing at him again, she hated him almost as much as she loved him because he made no effort to meet her half way. He just sat staring at her while continuing with his meal, indifferently.

'It's enough,' he raised his glass consideringly, his eyes mocking. 'How about you telling me something for a change?'

'Such as?'

'Such as how do you like living on St Lusanda?'

'I haven't been bored, if that's what you mean.'

'Strange,' his brow creased, as if he actually was puzzled. 'What have you been doing with yourself?'

'Nothing much, I'm afraid.' She always felt guilty about having nothing to do. 'Josephine and her family take care of everything. I insist on making my own bed . . .'

'Ours—after this,' Rick promised softly, as her voice trailed off.

The colour ran enchantingly under her clear skin as

she blushed. She knew a moment's blind panic when she wanted to jump to her feet and rush upstairs to her room. But this, as a sanctuary was no longer available and she didn't know where else she could go. Taking another quick gulp of her wine, she sensed his sardonic amusement and was aware of a sudden urge to get under his skin for a change.

'I wonder that you feel inclined to share your bed with a girl like me.'

'You asked me that before,' he sounded bored. 'Do I have to repeat I have little choice? You're my wife, after all, and there are no other girls here. Now finish your wine,' he commanded abruptly, as though the subject was closed.

Heedless with despair she did as she was told then rose unsteadily to her feet. He knew, she suspected, that she'd had a little too much. She wasn't used to anything more than the occasional glass of sherry, but he made no comment as he followed her careful progress from the dining-room. At the farm she had never been offered anything. So, she thought mutinously, was it to be wondered at that a few glasses of wine went to her head? As she crossed to the lounge and sat down, she had no real feelings of regret. While she did feel slightly ashamed of herself, a muzzy head seemed much easier to endure than one which registered Rick's every move much too clearly.

Giggling a little, she sank on to the sofa, vaguely conscious that Rick was staring at her again, with his permanently narrowed eyes.

The fleeting humour that had touched her disappeared immediately. 'Don't worry, Rick. I'm not drunk, just a little lightheaded. I don't suppose Veronica ever gets this way?'

'Leave her out of it,' he gave her a cup of very black coffee. 'You wouldn't be jealous?'

'A lot of good it would do me if I was,' she muttered,

broodingly. 'You'd be the one to get pleasure from seeing me suffer.'

'Perhaps,' he agreed callously. 'But right now I have no wish to see you suffering from anything. It might only lead to my own frustration.' Placing his own coffee on the mantelshelf of the huge fireplace he was standing beside, he regarded Emma with cool detachment. 'Drink your coffee, that should help. It's getting late.'

That was true. She had taken a long time over her dinner, eating slowly and pushing the food on her plate around with her fork, as though subconsciously seeking to prolong the evening indefinitely, to put off the moment she didn't want to think about. Now, when Rick mentioned that it was getting late, she fixed her attention on the empty fireplace rather than him. She had gazed too long at his dark, good-looking features over dinner, stared over deeply into his calculating blue eyes. That the blue had changed often almost to black with disapproval had made little difference. Her heart beat loudly and her limbs felt weak, her whole being drugged more by his hard attraction than anything else.

'Come here,' he said softly, as she met his eyes helplessly.

'No!' She stood up, suddenly completely in control of herself, tilting her chin. 'I'm going to bed, Rick—my own bed. You can find some other girl to tease.'

'I'm getting rapidly fed up,' his eyes hardened again as they went insolently over her. 'I don't intend going through this kind of charade every evening. From now on you'll do things my way—and stop arguing!'

Feeling altogether too apprehensive of him, Emma heard herself stammering an apology which she felt he didn't deserve. 'I'm sorry, Rick, I didn't mean to be annoying, but I would like to go to bed.'

'It's only ten,' he drawled tauntingly. 'You seem very eager.'

Only a minute ago he'd been saying it was late! 'I've

been in bed by ten since I came here,' she replied coldly. 'On the farm I always went early.'

'Always?' Sarcastically his thick brows rose. 'I can't believe Rex Oliver was such an early bird. It's not hard now to see what other men found so attractive, but you didn't always have such luscious curves.'

'Rex had nothing to do with it . . .'

'Hadn't he?' Rick snarled harshly, as she sought anxiously for words to explain. His hand caught her arm as she turned hopelessly away. Dragging her to him, he merely laughed when she winced, as his fingers gripped the bruise he had inflicted earlier.

As his arms closed ruthlessly around her, she cried, 'Please, Rick, let me go!'

'There's no point,' he drawled, his breath warm on her face. 'You're not going anywhere tonight, except with me.'

'Rick!' Anger gave way to a kind of desperate fear as she realised he was serious. 'How can you do this when you don't love me?'

'What has love to do with it?' he drawled, his glance going meaningfully over her. 'Don't tell me you've loved every man you've ever slept with?'

Tears clogged her throat with despair as she stared into his hard eyes, but before she could answer he caught her up. His arms going round her completely, he lifted her high against him, then crushed her trembling mouth beneath his own. Nor did he release her until she was trembling all over and the fists she had used to fight him with had uncurled and were finding their way blindly around his neck. Not until then did he stop kissing her, and when he did it was only to allow his lips to caress her tear-damp cheeks and her throat. Deftly he undid the buttons at the top of her dress, taking no notice of either her tears or pleading cries.

Feeling his hands gain their objective, she almost died

with shame. It proved useless to struggle, so she had to endure⸺ hadn't she? Endure, while she tried to ignore the flickering flames of desire which appeared to be igniting in both of them simultaneously. Rick had scarcely moved, but there didn't seem any necessity for hurry. He was letting everything happen slowly, but it was all the more potent for that. Then he was striding with her towards the door, carrying her through it, up the stairs to his bedroom. She might have weighed no more than a few pounds, and there was no help for her in the silent, sleeping house.

Inside the room, he dropped her to her feet and quietly closed the door, but just as she was thinking he might intend letting her go, he caught her to him again. Again she tried to fight as she felt him pulling her towards him, as she felt the hard muscles of his legs tense against the slimness of her own and he made no attempt to hide his rising desire. Though shocked at her own overwhelming response she was unable to resist him and stood shivering within his embrace, her head bent. As his hands slid from her ribcage to her hips, her body seemed to move towards him of its own accord. Then there was nothing but the warmth and hardness of him as his arms tightened and his mouth brushed her half hidden cheek.

The touch of his mouth brought reason back briefly. 'Rick,' she whispered, 'please don't!'

Harshly he laughed. 'That isn't what you said to Miles Ray.'

'Why won't you believe me, Rick?' Emma looked up at him, her eyes full of tears.

Again the harshness of his laughter made her close her eyes against it, as his hands went ruthlessly to her full breasts. 'There are certain signs that you've already given yourself to him. Signs I'd be a fool to ignore.'

Confused, she bit back a sob, half believing she would wake any moment to find this was all part of a bad dream.

Surely none of this could be happening to Emma Davis, who had never been out with a man in her life? Apart from her husband, who was convinced she was a girl who slept around.

'I know,' she gulped, 'that the evidence against me might look black, but if you'd only trust me!'

'Trust you!' his teeth nipped her earlobe derisively. 'You'll have to do better than that, I'm afraid.'

Fire leapt with pain from his teeth, making her cry out wildly, 'Why don't you ask Miles, Rick? He'd tell you the truth.'

'You must think me a fool,' he snapped. 'He's already had you and now he'd like to marry you, but don't imagine it's because he loves you.'

'What other reason could there be?'

'He might just wish to fulfil a lifelong ambition to get even with me.'

'Why should he want to do that?' she frowned.

'Because I've always managed to do better than he has, or so he thinks. To steal my wife, who he no doubt imagines is my pride and joy, would give his self-confidence a hell of a boost.'

'But why me?' Helplessly Emma shook her head. 'I'm so plain . . .'

'Not now, you aren't, my love.' Rick's voice was silky again as his eyes went over her. 'You've developed mysteriously while I've been away into quite something, even if your particular kind of beauty doesn't appeal to me. You still have that look of untouched innocence, and I hate pretence!'

He certainly knew how to wound! Tears ran down her face as he began ruthlessly to slide her dress from her shoulders, burying his mouth in her bare skin as he did so. She made one last attempt to rally some strength to fight him as her body went weak. 'Don't do anything you might regret, Rick.'

'To hell with that!' he said curtly, his mouth burning the vulnerable curve of her young throat. 'Aren't I entitled to demand my rights, take what I've already paid for?'

'You're taking . . .' she choked incoherently, 'and you aren't entitled to anything.'

'I won't take anything you aren't prepared to give.' His breathing had deepened, but he still spoke suavely.

Her heart racing, Emma realised it was the devil in him talking, the pitiless, cynical business man against whom she would never stand a chance. Already he had her subdued by his experienced caresses while her foolish body clamoured for more. She was dazed by the feelings it seemed he could so easily arouse in her. With a sense of dismay she acknowledged that she wanted him to make love to her, in the fullest sense of the word.

Foolishly, as such wanton yearnings began to really frighten her, she tried again to escape him. This brought his anger immediately down on her head. His jaw muscles tensed and his eyes hardened.

'Don't try me too far,' he rasped, his mouth claiming hers inexorably.

Determined to fight on, she clenched her lips tightly, which appeared to madden him. Lifting his hand, he caught her chin, holding her still while his cruel mouth forced hers open under his, controlling it so ruthlessly she couldn't do anything but submit. For a moment she managed a token resistance, raking his shoulders under his unbuttoned shirt, but he was too strong for her. He held her implacably until her mouth softened voluntarily and she went limp in his arms. Until the hands which attacked him began to cling instead of wounding, and the whole of her slender, shaking frame became helplessly responsive.

It was then, with a grunt of satisfaction, that he lifted her, laying her on the bed. Another minute and he was lying beside her, threading his fingers through her long, shining hair, his kisses hardening and lengthening into passion. He had all the expertise, while Emma was completely at the mercy of her emotions. As she dimly realised this, like someone drowning and coming up for the third time, a wild sob of protest choked in her throat and she twisted frantically away. She seemed to hit the peak of bitter humiliation when Rick's caressing hands soon had her turning back to him, her senses swimming, every inclination to struggle forgotten.

'Have you finished fighting me?' he muttered thickly, pushing her back against the pillows so he could see her face.

Emma found she couldn't answer. He was leaning on one elbow, staring at her, making her heart race so madly she didn't think she could have spoken coherently if she'd tried. Rick hadn't put on the light, but the moon shining in through the window was more than sufficient. Through dazed eyes she saw the broad strength of his shoulders, the powerful lines of his waist and thighs. Her cheeks went hot, but her eyes lingered in wonder as she realised he had nothing on.

She had never been as close to a man before, but all men, she knew, wouldn't be like this. She tried to be angry with herself that an awakening delight in his undoubted masculinity was rapidly replacing a sense of shame. How could she even begin to feel this way when as soon as he could Rick would be getting rid of her? She loved him, but she mustn't use this as an excuse for surrendering herself so easily. Yet what else could she do? What else did she really want to do? Might not this be all she would ever have to remember? That once she had actually appealed to him so much he had wanted her?

With a sigh, she nodded weakly to his query, letting her arms creep eagerly around his neck. When he muttered hoarsely, 'I hope I don't disappoint you,' she

tried not to think of how different it might have been if
instead he had whispered words of love. Then such a
coming together could only have held sheer joy.

Yet when his mouth began moving insistently over hers,
the renewed, frantic beat of her heart and racing pulse
stifled any more regrets. As her lips parted and she clung
to him, she shivered as she felt his passion growing. He
wasn't treating her as a novice. Dimly she understood
that he expected to find her almost as experienced as
himself, and having had no experience at all, Emma could
only let her senses guide her. These, however, seemed
swiftly to let her down. Soon she was twisting and gasping
in his arms, apprehension mixing with excitement to such
a degree it appeared to be removing any pleasure.
Nevertheless, although she scarcely knew what she was
doing, she couldn't seem to get close enough to the man
who was so frightening her.

His broad chest hurt, but when she tried to protest he
punished her by letting her feel the full weight of his thighs
over hers, before he moved in to take total possession. She
was crushed and crying out, rent with pain—yet transported, was it seconds or minutes later? to unknown
heights. Enmeshed by her own emotions, she was battered
by the strength of Rick's hard, male body, his harsh rasp-
ing breath. She was fleeing from yet racing towards incredulous delight, then clinging to him while trying to
push him away. She was terrified to grasp what was within
her reach, but unable to prevent herself—in the final out-
come, from being utterly consumed by the ultimate rap-
ture.

CHAPTER NINE

AFTERWARDS, Emma was aware only of a curious exhaustion. The fires which had consumed her were still smouldering but slowly dying down, leaving her with a sensation which was far from unpleasant—which normally, she suspected, would have left her on the brink of sleep, in the arms of her lover. She was therefore confused to find herself sobbing.

It must, she thought, her hot cheeks growing cold with unhappiness, be Rick's heavy silence which was affecting her so. It seemed to condemn her in a way she failed to understand. Obviously she had failed to please him and he wasn't prepared to make any allowance for her lack of experience. Of course, she reminded herself, he thought she had been around, so no doubt he believed she had been deliberately reticent with him. Unable to even guess the depth of her own response, she imagined he had a legitimate cause for complaint, and her sense of misery increased when he didn't speak. She was desolate that he should be considering the delight she imagined they had shared in such stony silence.

Feeling suddenly ill, she slipped blindly from the bed. Stumbling frantically towards the bathroom, she was startled but strangely unheeding to find herself immediately lifted in Rick's arms and carried there.

'Be quiet,' he commanded tersely as she tried to protest. Through eyes bright with tears, she noticed irrationally his face was white.

Later he carried her back to bed again and gently wiped the tears from her cheeks. Surprised at how gentle his hands could be, she wanted to thank him, but the gratitude in her eyes was hidden by eyelids suddenly too heavy to raise and her voice was somehow non-existent. Reaction, now fast setting in, caused her to lie still and pale, completely unresistant as Rick covered her with a light sheet. Again he was gentle. Briefly she fancied his hand trembled as he brushed a loose strand of hair from off her hot forehead. His touch was so tender that she turned her mouth blindly into his palm as he caressed her cheek. But just as she tried to whisper how much she loved him, she fell asleep.

He was gone next morning when she woke. Lying in a kind of daze, she thought of him, trying to put together, like pieces of a jigsaw, a clear picture of everything that had happened. Needless to say she failed. Much of the puzzle, no matter how hard she tried, just wouldn't fall into place.

The last half hour, before sleep had overtaken her, Emma found easiest to recall—perhaps because her mind shied nervously away from everything else. Surely Rick couldn't hate her too much, for hadn't he taken care of her as compassionately as any woman? His face had been grim, his eyes bleak, but he hadn't been obviously disgusted at the way she had trembled and shivered, and been unable to help herself in the bathroom. He had done everything for her that she hadn't been able to do for herself, and she didn't think she had thanked him. If only he had been here now, she might have thought of a way.

Her cheeks hot, she turned to bury her face briefly in her pillow. This was Rick's bed and she suddenly knew she wanted to stay in it. When he had invited her to, she had refused, but when she saw him she would tell him she had changed her mind. This morning it might be possible to tell him a lot of things she had felt reluctant to even mention last night.

Trembling, she recalled how he had made love to her, yet still found it impossible to recapture one perfectly lucid moment. The electricity that existed between them had leapt without restraint, as if along bare wires. Emma doubted if either of them could have prevented what had happened. It had been so fierce it had seemed to take the last of Rick's control.

She thought she remembered exactly when he lost it, the moment when his arms had tightened savagely and she had gasped against the increasing pressure of his mouth. Feverishly now she wished she could recall the whole of it, but certain parts of the night were still shrouded in a peculiar darkness.

By the time she had showered and dressed Rick still hadn't come, as she had half expected he would to see what she was doing. Thinking he must be busy in his office and forgotten how late it was, she went downstairs in search of him. Finding him neither in the office or the dining-room, she ran along to the kitchen where Josephine told her he had gone out.

'Boss always busy on Lusanda,' she trilled, glancing curiously at Emma's stricken face as she prepared the young mistress some fresh coffee.

Belasco walked in, almost ready, from the look of him to leave for Barbados. 'Just in time to say goodbye, little missus,' he grinned.

Little—missus? Emma stared at him sharply. He hadn't called her that since the day he had met her, when she had stepped off the plane. 'Have you seen Rick?' she asked, disregarding Josephine's eloquent eyes.

'Boss on the other side of the island,' Belasco replied, the expression on his face making her heart suddenly sink.

Stubbornly, Emma kept a bright smile fixed on her face. 'I'll have my breakfast and then see if I can find him.'

'He isn't in a good mood this morning,' Belasco said carefully. Emma felt he was trying to warn her of something. 'Better wait here until he gets back, this evening.'

Emma was aware of the coldness of shock moving slowly

through her. So it was to be exactly as it had been on Barbados? There, the only time she had seen Rick was at dinner. Unless Belasco was mistaken. Perhaps it didn't do to be too hasty. Rick couldn't have forgotten what had taken place between them so quickly. A man, she knew, had his work to do, but on this one morning, surely, Rick wouldn't put work before everything else?

Yet for all her brief optimism there was no real hope in her heart as she said goodbye to Belasco and tried to eat some of the appetising breakfast which Josephine cooked for her. And for the remainder of the day, as she waited in vain for Rick, her heart grew heavier. What a fool she had been to imagine he cared! Hadn't he warned her he was only interested in one thing and, in her case, it was merely because he believed she had been having affairs with other men. Maybe it was a good thing he had gone. At least it had given her time to think—otherwise she might have foolishly confessed that she loved him.

She lay on the beach, but felt too listless to swim. After lunch she went upstairs and sat on the bed, but that led her to wonder what Rick would think if he was to return unexpectedly and find her there. Did she really want to look like a slave girl waiting for her master? Flushing at her own stupidity, she went down to the beach again and because of her aching head lay down under one of the numerous palm trees, where she eventually fell asleep.

Later she stirred herself and went back to the house to change for dinner. She wore a pale silky dress in which she looked beautiful, although she hurried more than usual so as to be downstairs before Rick arrived. If he did come. Perhaps he had gone with Belasco and she would be none the wiser until he sent a message from Barbados?

When he walked in, half an hour later, she was leafing through the same magazine for the umpteenth time and beginning to feel sick with worry. She tried to smile, but her face felt stiff. Her must have entered the house the back way, as she often did herself, and had obviously showered and changed. Emma didn't allow her glance to linger more than seconds on the well-fitting black pants, tightly belted to lean, powerful hips. Her breath catching, she remembered how they had felt moving against her and hastily raised her eyes higher, to his cool, open-necked shirt.

'Have you had a good day?' she managed, rather acidly, as he nodded in brief acknowledgement to her travesty of a smile and went to pour himself a drink.

'Not really,' he replied, tautly she thought, as if Belasco's dry observation had been correct and he was definitely in a bad mood. As she frowned over this, she heard him say, 'And you?'

'Belasco left,' she replied dully, 'and I went down to the beach.' Flushing painfully, because even now she could scarcely bring herself to look at him calmly, she added, 'There seemed nothing else to do.'

Glancing at her quickly, Rick threw back his whisky in one go, pouring himself another. 'You sound bored?'

When she didn't reply, he glanced at her sharply again and appeared to remember he hadn't offered her anything. When she declined a dry sherry he didn't persist, but his mouth tightened as she shook her head.

Emma knew it must seem as if she was acting childishly, but she feared a drink might give her the kind of courage she could well do without. Whatever happened, she mustn't risk a repetition of last night, not when Rick obviously despised her. Why should he think she was bored? Was he offering her an excuse to leave the island? Well, he could go and jump in the lagoon! she thought rebelliously. She liked St Lusanda and she was staying!

Her small face mutinously set, she assured him she was never bored. 'I told you I like it here,' she said, doing her best to meet his dark, watchful eyes, so he would know she meant it.

To her surprise he drew a deep breath and offered, almost lightly, 'Tomorrow, if you like, I'll take you sailing. We can take our lunch and relax, I believe it might do us both good.'

What was he playing at, or who with? Emma had no wish to be mouse to his cat. She distrusted the almost eager glint in his eyes. It confused her as much as the hint of anxiety when she hesitated. 'Won't you be too busy to spare the time?' she asked stiffly.

He frowned, his face paling, a muscle twitching at the side of his mouth. 'Maybe I deserved that,' he muttered grimly, 'but I had a lot to think about today. It—it hasn't been easy.'

As she had never heard his decisive voice falter before, Emma's eyes widened. For no reason she could think of, hot colour flooded her cheeks, and because it embarrassed her, she found herself persisting irrationally, 'Should you be wasting time going sailing?'

'Do you know,' he teased, some of the brief tension leaving his face, 'you're beginning to sound like a nagging wife already!'

Her eyes puzzled, she gazed back at him. He was suddenly smiling and talking quite naturally, if with a hint of forced determination which she couldn't quite fathom. He was like a man who had set himself a course and was doing his best to stick to it, regardless of his deeper inclinations. Yet when intuitively she sensed he was begging her to meet him halfway, she dismissed it as nonsense. Hadn't that been her trouble all along? Wasn't she forever imagining he was changing towards her? Men like Rick Conway were too arrogant to beg. In her case, probably all he was after was a kind of unarmed truce until they parted. Knowing this, Emma felt a great reluctance to spend the next day with him. He was a man who never missed a thing, and she might so easily betray her love.

It seemed less than sensible, after working this all out,

to find herself agreeing to go with him, without further argument. Her only consolation lay in the fact that she managed to speak coolly.

She also managed to listen coolly, when he spent the next hour discussing where they might go and what they might do. For the rest of the evening he bewildered her greatly, for while he made no attempt to touch her he rarely removed his eyes from her strained young face. After making every decision possible about the proposed trip, he took her in to dinner, during which he told her twice she looked beautiful—and in such a way that she found it difficult to believe he wasn't sincere. Afterwards he surprised her even more by playing her favourite records and talking to her at length about Canada.

It might have been a perfect evening if he had come up to bed with her. This Emma admitted to herself with burning cheeks. But at eleven he merely noted that if they were to make an early start it was time girls of her age retired. He said he had work to do and would be up later, but although she lay for a long time in the bed they shared, waiting and wondering, he never came. When she woke in the morning there was no imprint of his head on the other pillows, and she wondered if he had slept downstairs or if he had continued working throughout the night.

If Rick had worked all night he looked remarkably fit when she met him downstairs for breakfast. For a moment she panicked at the sight of him. He was clad only in a faded blue denim shirt and matching shorts, and she felt herself responding almost helplessly to a sense of shared sensuality. For a bewildering moment she knew a practically irresistible longing to be in his arms and had to turn away before he guessed at the emotions which threatened to tear her apart. It didn't help, somehow, that when she regained control and turned back to him, his eyes, when they met hers, appeared to be smouldering.

As they set off across the bay, Emma wondered why she had worried so much about the trip. They were not alone. The young man who had been Belasco's assistant was with them and although he kept at a discreet distance she was always conscious of his presence.

'Why did you bring him?' she asked Rick impulsively.

'For the ride,' he replied tightly, but as she shrank from him he controlled his anger. 'I'm sorry, Emma.'

Not at all enlightened, she glanced at him, frowning, noting suddenly the lines of strain around his mouth and eyes. 'Didn't you get any sleep at all last night? I listened, but I never heard you come upstairs.'

Flushing hotly, she regretted her impulsive tongue when she saw his eyes darken with a renewed flicker of the flame which had unnerved her earlier. But he merely said, 'There was too much to do.'

'Doesn't your overseer do most of it?' Thoughtfully Emma studied the blue horizon. 'He called at the house a few days ago and had coffee with me. He seems a very nice and efficient young man.'

'You didn't mention that,' Rick said curtly.

'I must have forgotten,' she replied uncertainly.

His voice hardened. 'Well . . . next time he calls you aren't at home. Not that he will be calling again!' he added, with cold emphasis.

Unhappily Emma bit her full bottom lip to stop it trembling, but was unable to do anything about the sudden tears in her eyes. 'You'll never learn to trust me, will you, Rick?'

'Oh, hell!' he muttered, half under his breath, his jaw tight with a kind of self-derision. Then, making a visible effort to check a further release of his feelings, he spoke more rationally. 'It's not you I wouldn't trust, Emma.'

While her colour deepened again, his eyes went closely over the full curves of her slender young figure, as if he never wanted to look elsewhere. Savagely, although his voice was low, he exclaimed, 'My memory will take me back as far as two nights ago, you know. I can remember the feel and taste of you. I can understand how any man might find you irresistible. And you have to believe that once he's tasted the honey a man might become maddened for more.'

As his voice roughened, Emma began trembling, as a strange heat invaded her limbs. Rick looked as though he would liked to have carried on where he'd left off and, as if she had no will of her own to resist him, she took an involuntary step towards him.

The tenseness of her face, the shaken way in which she uttered his name, appeared to bring him to his senses. It was obvious he thought he had frightened her and he placed a reassuring hand on her arm. 'I'm sorry, Emma,' the chiselled planes of his face relaxed slightly, into wry cynicism, 'I seem to be letting myself get carried away. Why don't we concentrate on learning to be friends for a change? We might even find we like each other.'

Shaking her head blindly, Emma turned and stumbled away from him to the other side of the launch. Didn't he realise she loved him? Learning to like him didn't come into it. Already, although she couldn't be sure exactly when it had happened, she was hopelessly committed. Now, if she had to learn to do anything, it would have to be how to do without him, when he sent her away.

Rick didn't follow her unsteady flight, but a few minutes later he called that coffee was ready. Grateful for his tact, that he had given her time to pull herself together, she managed to return to his side with a relatively easy smile. After this the day passed without incident, the only other slight crack in the even tenor of it occurring when Rick came to help her remove her snorkel after they had been exploring the reefs.

They had anchored in a bay off the shore of a deserted island where the beaches were pink and white and around the exotic coral reefs the water went down, crystal clear to a depth of over a hundred feet. About an hour after lunch they left Dan in charge of the boat while Rick had shown her an underwater world of such beauty it had left her dazed. Perhaps this was why, after leaving the water, she fumbled so much with her equipment that he was forced to come to her assistance.

Clearly having no wish to touch her if he could avoid it, he sighed impatiently. 'Come here and let me see what you're doing. I never knew such a child for getting in trouble!'

Emma submitted with ill grace as he completed in a few seconds what she hadn't been able to accomplish in as many minutes. 'Do you always have to be so superior, Rick?'

'I am superior,' he tapped the tip of her delightful nose lightly, 'and don't you forget it!'

'Women are equal,' she dared protest.

'Not my women,' he taunted. 'Certainly not my wife.'

Briefly, as her eyes dropped from the intentness of his, she let her glance roam over him, allowing herself the luxury that wouldn't be hers much longer. He was so tall and broad and so virile. She supposed he wasn't strictly handsome, but his features were so rugged and dominating he could make most other men seem effeminate by comparison.

'Rick,' she breathed, suddenly forgetting everything but that they were alone together, her voice suddenly husky.

He in turn was also doing some slow surveying. Emma's bikini was brief, but he had no obvious compunction in letting his gaze strip what there was of it so that he might explore the creamy fulness of the rose-tipped curves which lay under the two wet triangles of thin cotton. Suddenly she found herself in his arms, his breath warm on her face, while his bare muscled thigh pressed against hers making her aware of the way she was arousing him.

His hand slid in circles to caress her sunwarmed shoulder as he bent with a thick exclamation to find her mouth. Her protective instincts did react feebly, but these he overwhelmed easily merely by increasing the pressure of his demanding lips. She felt her blood race, her senses spin as he drew her so close she felt she must be welded to every muscle and sinew of his hard body. Her lips parted under the insistence of his, and while her mind reeled she knew intuitively that he wanted her. Wanted her so badly that she suspected if Dan hadn't been near he would have taken her there and then.

Burying his face in the warm curve of her neck, he thrust her bikini top aside with skilled fingers. Then, as his mouth dropped lower to explore the thrusting softness of her breasts, her nails dug wantingly into the sweat-damp skin of his broad back. Pushing his hands through her long, loose hair, he held her fiercely, so that she felt the drag of his teeth on her throbbing skin.

Then, as she shuddered convulsively, he gave a muffled groan and she was free. It happened so quickly she was unable immediately to do anything but force open heavy lashes to stare at him. Because there seemed no reason for his sudden rejection, she whispered beseechingly, 'Why, Rick?'

For a moment he hesitated, his eyes on her unsteady mouth. 'There are reasons,' he replied bleakly, his jaw taut.

One of those reasons could be Veronica? And whatever else it had been, Emma felt she should be grateful that something had prompted him to let her go. How could she have been about to surrender herself to him again so easily when he had never come near her since making love to her the other night? Her cheeks cold with a painful humiliation, she glanced blindly towards the boat.

'I think I see Dan waving,' she improvised, not caring whether Rick believed her or not. He might be just as glad as she was of an excuse to leave.

He appeared to be. 'We'd better get back,' he agreed tightly, on a note of anger that made Emma flinch.

Oddly hurt by it, she began hurrying towards the rubber dinghy in which Rick had brought them ashore.

'Hadn't you better get dressed?' he called after her curtly. And, as she spun around on a gasp, 'Not that your shorts are much of an improvement on what you're wearing, but they might at least deter Dan from attempting to push me overboard and having his way with you.'

Feeling he was making a visible effort to lighten the atmosphere, rather than being dog in the mangerish, Emma tried to meet him halfway but failed. The careless rejoinder she sought failed to materialise. Bitterly she heard herself saying instead, 'Would any man want a girl like me?'

His face hardened, but almost as if he welcomed her antagonism. 'I think we have some evidence of that.'

'Evidence!' she laughed, her eyes suddenly wild as she didn't pretend to misunderstand him. 'Ben, who vowed he loved me yet went off without even saying goodbye, and Miles Ray, who also swore he loved me but hasn't made any attempt that I can see to rescue me.'

'Did you give him an excuse to? Didn't you ever pretend you loved him?'

Emma went white and this time didn't answer. What was the use of denying it? Hadn't she done so, without success, again and again?'

'Forget it, Emma.' Staring at her closely, Rick sighed heavily, his face almost as pale as her own. 'That's not a question I should have asked as I already know the answer. I seem to have made, and am still making, one hell of a mess of things.'

Dan looked as though the approaching dinghy had just woken him up. He was surprised that they wanted to leave so early. Grumbling goodnaturedly, he stirred himself reluctantly.

'We can always come back,' Rick said carefully, watching Emma's wistful face as they set off.

'How long will we be staying on St Lusanda?' she shrugged, trying to pretend she didn't care whether they came back or not.

'That depends,' he frowned.

'On what, for heaven's sake?' Deliberately she made her voice querulous. 'If we're going to be divorced, wouldn't it be wiser if we separated as soon as possible?'

In savage undertones, so Dan wouldn't hear, Rick retorted tightly, 'Separate rooms separate lives. Is that what you really want?'

'You insisted on that from the beginning,' she stammered angrily, refusing to let herself imagine he suddenly didn't want these things himself.

His eyes flashed. 'And when I dragged you into my room, did you like what I did to you?' The question seemed torn out of him and there was a white ring around his mouth.

How could a girl answer that, when the very air was cold with hostility? On the night he mentioned Emma had been in both heaven and hell. The other way round, she corrected herself numbly. It was torture, the subsequent longing she was swamped with to repeat the experience. Her only comfort was that Rick didn't know. Nor must he guess! 'I can't remember,' she lied.

'Am I supposed to be flattered?' he grated. 'I know exactly how you feel. You don't have to spell it out. You can return to your old room tonight and I promise never to enter it again.'

If this reduced Emma to silent misery for the rest of the journey, a fresh shock awaited her as they approached St Lusanda. There on the jetty stood Gail and Veronica. Gail was waving, but Veronica was not.

Emma went cold all over and swayed. Veronica hadn't wasted much time, she thought bitterly. Rick was staring at the two girls almost as hard as she was, but she couldn't tell what he was thinking.

As Dan, showing off before his glamorous audience, circled widely, Emma murmured foolishly, 'Veronica and Gail . . .'

'Yes,' Rick snapped tersely, cautioning Dan. Rick frowned. He looked impatient, a slight flush lying over his high cheekbones. Suddenly he turned to Emma, meeting her anxious eyes. 'We have to talk,' he said urgently, 'very soon.'

Because of Veronica. Dully Emma gazed at him, painfully reluctant to ask in so many words. He must be desperately worried for fear Veronica should discover what had happened between him and his wife. Didn't he know she would never betray him? She might be a fool, but she could never do that.

'Soon,' he insisted, apparently not sure if she had heard him.

'I suppose so.' She averted her eyes quickly so he shouldn't see her tears. 'Will—will they be staying long?'

'I shouldn't think so,' he replied indifferently.

Emma, wishing he hadn't left her with the impression that as far as he was concerned they were welcome to stay as long as they liked, bent her head and said nothing more.

'Where on earth have you been, darling?' Veronica, quite definitely annoyed, frowned on Rick as he leapt lithely onto the jetty. 'You told me you would be working,' she added accusingly.

'A man has to have an occasional day off.' He suffered Gail's sisterly peck on his cheek, but Emma noticed he did nothing to evade Veronica's more enthusiastic greeting.

It made Emma stumble as she tried to leave the boat

unaided; it was only Dan's quick reaction which prevented her from falling. As he grabbed hold of her she glanced at him gratefully.

'I'll see to my wife.' Looking distinctly annoyed, Rick removed her from Dan's protective arms, picking her up and carrying her on shore himself. The way he held her was strangely possessive, Emma realised, and she might have enjoyed it if it hadn't been for the smear of Veronica's lipstick across his mouth.

'Are you all right?' he asked, his eyes on her pale face as he slowly set her down.

'Yes, thank you,' she answered, slightly breathless. Rick kept his arms around her, as if making sure. She was aware that both Gail and Veronica were staring at her too. Their frowning glances were roving her sand-hazed limbs, bare beneath brief shorts. The shorts and equally brief top made her appear small and slender. Unaware that the shape underneath was decidedly sexy, she wondered why Veronica continued to look so disapproving.

Gail, conscious of Rick's grim expression, removed her curious gaze from Emma and asked tentatively, 'You don't mind us coming over, do you, Rick?'

'Of course he doesn't!' Veronica brushed such a suggestion aside with cast-iron confidence. 'You did say I could come any time, didn't you, darling?' she smiled charmingly at Rick.

'Did I?' he said dryly, retaining his hold of Emma though she twisted to escape him. His fingers, as though to punish her, dug deeper into her narrow waist and she was still.

Veronica gushed on. 'It's been so dull on Barbados while you've been in Canada, darling, and you were only home a few days when you rushed over here. After we had dinner together the other night, I just knew I couldn't bear to let you out of my sight again.'

Feeling sick, Emma pulled herself from Rick's grasp,

this time succeeding. Ready to flee because of the deluge of misery that hit her, she had to remind herself severely of several things, Rick wasn't her property, so it was no use feeling ill every time she was made to remember this. But how could he have made love to her, as he had done, practically straight from the arms of another woman?

With eyes suddenly wet with tears, which she didn't really care if anyone noticed, she stared at him contempt-uously. Like most men, he obviously didn't appreciate having his affairs brought so blatantly into the open. But let him frown! He had nothing to look so tight-lipped about, surely? Not with Veronica looking ready to melt in his arms, her eyes more openly inviting by the minute.

Veronica talked all the way back to the house, ignoring Emma, even when Rick, surprisingly, kept his wife firmly by his side in the station wagon. Emma, feeling his hard, muscled thigh pressing against hers, wondered, from the glint in his eyes, if he was teasing her deliberately. Nervously she caught her breath at the surge of fiery sen-sation and had to remind herself that he was probably only trying to make Veronica jealous.

'May I choose my own room, darling?' Veronica turned beguilingly to Rick as they left the vehicle and entered the hallway. 'Not too far from yours, I think, in case I get scared during the night. Remote islands can be frighten-ing after dark.'

Emma didn't think Veronica had ever been scared in her life. If she went searching for Rick in the night it wouldn't be for that kind of help. She clearly believed Rick didn't sleep with his wife, and Emma's cheeks flushed painfully when she realised only Rick could have told her.

She was about to speak angrily, and, for once, without discretion, when Rick said coolly, 'There are two rooms at the top of the stairs, Veronica. You and Gail can have those. Mine is much farther along the corridor.'

'Oh, but . . .'

'They're the only rooms available for guests,' he assured her, 'if you intend staying.'

Instantly, as his voice hardened, Veronica was all charming capitulation. 'Of course, they'll do fine, Rick. Does it matter where we sleep?'

Where we sleep? Veronica's words held a soft insinuation which made Emma flinch unhappily. Yet surely Rick wouldn't attempt to carry on a clandestine relationship with another woman, with his wife in the same house? All the same, even the thought of it disturbed her, making her realise more than ever how desperately she loved him.

'Excuse me,' she stammered, avoiding the narrowed glitter in Rick's dark eyes, 'I'd better go and tell Josephine there'll be two extra for dinner.'

Gail asked quickly, before Emma could move, 'Will your intriguing manager be joining us for dinner, Rick?'

'No! Well, why not?' Suddenly he appeared to change his mind, as he assessed Emma's taut face. 'If you think he might keep you amused, Gail, I'll send a message.'

After leaving the kitchen, Emma made her way upstairs. Her footsteps dragged and she felt curiously distraite. One half of her seemed numb, with a kind of fatalistic acceptance of the future, the other half ripped by what she suspected was not yet fully realised pain. She was relieved, on noticing the dark strain in her eyes in the mirror, that as Rick had to contact his manager she might have an hour to pull herself together.

When she came back from her bath, however, he was lounging on the bed. Immediately he rose to his feet, and crossed over to her.

'Emma,' he muttered, a finger going under her chin, 'I didn't mean things to happen this way. I would have spared you if I could.'

'Not at all,' she whispered stiffly, her eyes huge. 'It really doesn't matter.'

'Of course it matters!' he returned sharply, his fingers tightening on her fragile jawbone. 'Look, Emma, I know we haven't a lot of time, but we have to talk.'

'I'd—I'd rather not,' she replied, her voice low, her thick lashes fanning her cheeks to hide the ache in her heart which must surely be reflected in her eyes. 'Please, Rick, I don't think I could stand it. I've had just about enough!'

'You have?'

'Yes!' she gasped at the extreme curtness of his tones. 'I just want to be left alone . . .'

'So you can have an affair with Miles Ray?'

'No!'

'Little liar!' Anger flared in his eyes as he tilted the chin he held, so he could crush her petal-soft mouth under his as he lowered his head. When she kept her lips closed, he rubbed his mouth softly against hers until she opened them, allowing him access. Yet he didn't actually hurt her, not physically. Strangely she felt it was Rick who was suffering most. Incredibly he seemed to be trembling against her as he moulded her yielding softness to the hardening contours of his own strong body. He stirred in her a passion which seemed to be affecting him. Suddenly she was consumed by fire, a languorous yet urgent desire to be possessed by him, just once more . . .

'I'll leave you alone when I'm good and ready,' he growled thickly, 'and not before.'

CHAPTER TEN

As the gong in the hall rang piercingly through the house, Emma gasped and made a frantic effort to free herself.

'If you don't hurry you'll have Veronica searching for you, Rick,' she cried wildly, as his head jerked up.

'And you don't think she should catch me making love to my wife?' he mocked.

'That wasn't your intention.'

'Whatever my intention, in another moment I wouldn't have known what I was doing. Did you know that?' he retorted harshly. 'I believe you did. I also believe you wanted me almost as much as I did you.'

Tears burning the back of her eyes, Emma turned away. He was a virile, sensual man and had never tried to hide it. It might be a small feather in her cap that she did appear occasionally to succeed in arousing his passion, but it was his love she wanted most, and apparently Veronica had that.

Without answering, or glancing at him again, Emma swiftly grabbed the first dress she came to and locked herself in the bathroom. Here she completed a hasty toilet and when she came out again, Rick was gone.

When his overseer joined them they were all in the lounge. Larry Turner was young and handsome and it was quite clear that Gail liked him. Emma, feeling her heartbeats settling more evenly, stepped forward to speak to him. He seemed to represent everything that was normal, ordinary and sane, and because she felt oddly grateful there was perhaps more warmth than there should have been in her smile.

Rick, she suspected, had invited him mainly to remove

from his shoulders some of the burden of entertaining three young women on his own. But contrary to what was expected of him, Larry Turner seemed to concentrate almost solely on Emma, regardless of the growing disapproval in Rick's icy blue eyes.

Gail, not used to being practically ignored by a man who had taken her fancy, grew sulky, and Rick, as if aware of this, kept Emma firmly by his side. She sat by him during dinner and although he had little to say to her he was attentive, seeing to her every need. He even placed his hand over hers, as it lay on the table, playing idly with her fingers as he conversed lightly with the others. This, Emma realised, was to let Larry Turner know she wasn't available, and to help his sister. Knowing this, she mocked her racing pulse and told herself not to be so foolish.

She also felt very nervous when once or twice she encountered Veronica's vindictive stare. She was somehow sure that Veronica was tempted to speak of Miles, but the meal continued without him being mentioned. Veronica, though, must know about Miles and the mysterious appearance of his bracelet in Emma's room, and Emma had an uneasy feeling that the other girl was just biding her time.

After dinner Veronica and Gail demanded music and dancing, and Rick was seemingly willing enough to indulge them. As Larry hesitated between Gail and herself, Emma murmured a quick excuse and left the room. When she returned to the lounge she saw, with a sigh of relief, that he was dancing with Gail, but it wasn't relief she felt in her heart when she was forced to watch Veronica circling on the polished floor in Rick's arms. Veronica had her arms around his neck and was holding him tightly, while across the empty space between them Rick's eyes met Emma's enigmatically.

He didn't ask her to dance, but neither did he dance

again, and later, when Larry left and the three girls went upstairs he said he had some work to do in his study before he came to bed.

On the point of returning to her old room, Emma found herself hesitating. Rick had more or less given her permission to do so, but if he was again to spend most of the night in his study she saw no reason to go back to her own room immediately. Not even to herself would she admit that she was reluctant, in spite of everything, that Veronica should discover that Rick and she weren't sleeping together. Veronica's eyes had been extremely calculating as she had walked upstairs. Perhaps, Emma thought bitterly, both Rick and Veronica expected to find his room empty. Well, if they did they might be in for a surprise!

While it was easy enough to let a resurgence of pride and defiance persuade her to stay where she was, by the time Emma was undressed and into Rick's bed she was trembling so much with nervous reaction she found it impossible to sleep. Knowing she must pretend to be asleep, if he should happen to come upstairs, she listened anxiously for any sound of approaching footsteps. When, at the end of the corridor, she heard a door opening she was so agitated she had slipped out of bed to see who it was almost before she realised what she was doing. Quietly she opened her own door just in time to see Veronica disappearing downstairs.

Agony tearing at her heart, Emma went desolately back to bed. So much for her vague hopes that Rick's increased attentiveness this evening had meant something! He had said he had work to do, but it must all have been pretence. He was simply using work as an excuse to stay downstairs and see Veronica. Damn him and his women! First Blanche, now Veronica. How many more, Emma wondered, before and after and in between?

Her whole being aching with suppressed bitterness and

anger, she huddled miserably under the sheets. She wanted to cry, but the hurt went too deep, and hadn't she wept too much already? Dry-eyed, she lay with her eyes closed, as if that would shut out the mental picture she had of Rick in his study with another girl in his arms.

Then, as she lay rigid, not more than a few minutes later Rick came in. When the door opened Emma feared for a second it must be Veronica looking for him, but as he closed the door quietly and crossed to the bed she would have known his footsteps anywhere.

Pausing beside her, he softly spoke her name. When she didn't answer she heard him flinging off his clothes and then the sound of the shower in the bathroom before he returned and got in the other side of the bed. Obviously he had concluded that she was alseep, and although she was sure he must hear the loud thud of her heart, Emma continued to pretend she was.

As Rick made no attempt to speak again or to touch her, after a while she risked a quick peep. He was lying on his back, well away from her, his eyes open, gazing towards the window. His profile was remote in the dim light, but as he didn't turn his head she knew he wasn't aware of her furtive glances.

If Veronica had found him, their meeting must have been extremely brief, too brief for anything to have happened. Emma sighed with a kind of blissful relief. She longed to have Rick reach out and put his arms around her, but she was suddenly so wonderfully comforted by his very presence that her other desires didn't seem so urgent any more. There was such intense happiness to be found in the knowledge that he was here with her and not with someone else. Slowly she felt herself relax until, worn out by her emotions and the tensions of a long, tiring day, she was suddenly asleep.

Through the night she dreamt she had snuggled closer and Rick's arms were about her, holding her tightly.

Faintly she heard him soothing her restlessness with tender yet rueful words, as though he shared that same restlessness himself. She seemed to feel his hands quietly carressing her, lulling her until her sleep deepened, and for the first time in weeks her mind and slender body were utterly at peace.

It was after nine next morning when she woke to find Rick gently shaking her. 'Wake up, lazybones,' he was saying softly.

'Rick?' her sleepy eyes opened wide with dismay as she struggled to sit up. 'What time is it?'

'For you,' he smiled, 'that doesn't matter. But I have a lot to arrange. I have to go out.'

While she heard this it didn't really register. She was only conscious that he was here beside her, staring at her enigmatically as he sat on the edge of the bed.

'You slept with me—last night?' she whispered, involuntarily.

'Yes.' His hand fell on her bare shoulder as his eyes glinted teasingly. 'I suspected you knew.' Ignoring her resultant confusion, he dropped a swift kiss on her startled lips. 'If you were to ask me nicely, I might even do it again.'

This, seeming too much to assimilate immediately, left her stammering nervously, 'I—I must have slept well.'

'You did,' he muttered threateningly. 'Better than you might do in future—unless you want me wild with frustration.'

'Rick?' She swallowed, scarcely able to meet the smouldering darkness in his eyes with any equanimity. 'Why are you being like this?'

His eyes narrowed, his face hardening as he rose swiftly to his feet. 'I'll explain later. We'll talk later.' His voice was suddenly terse as he bent down to smooth a hand almost tenderly over her rumpled mass of gleaming hair. 'When we do I want all the time in the world. So first I have to get all my other problems sorted out. If I stop with you now I might never get round to them. Until then, trust me.'

A bewildered cry escaped Emma as she watched him stride through the door, but he didn't turn. What had he meant? How could she be sure she had heard him properly? Had he really talked as if he cared for her? Might she not be a fool to take him seriously? Her heart turned over at the possibility of his being in love with her. Her stomach churned even harder when she tried to consider what this could mean. Or—she pulled herself off cloud nine with difficulty—was this merely a ruse to make Veronica jealous? Had they quarrelled last night and was Rick just pretending to care for his wife so as to make Veronica jealous? So many questions presented themselves that Emma grew confused, because she didn't know the answers.

Yet, as she climbed out of bed, the glow in her heart refused to be suppressed altogether and a new, tentative optimism swept much of her depression aside. Swiftly she dressed and went downstairs to find the others. The house, however, was empty and she couldn't see anything of Gail or Veronica outside. Josephine shook her head when she went to the kitchen to see if they were there.

'Those girls aren't kitchen birds, little missus. You wouldn't find them chatting up old Jo. No, child, they're still in bed, and I'm letting them sleep.'

'I expect they're tired.' Emma, continuing to feel happy, could have found an excuse for the devil that morning. Softly she smiled and with renewed appetite tackled her breakfast. She had two cups of coffee and ate several of Josephine's delicious croissants, warm from the oven and dripping with honey. She laughed when the honey trickled over her lips. She fancied if Rick had been there he might have licked it off. He might even have carried her back to bed and finished the job off there, although she doubted if he would have been satisfied with only the honey.

Her cheeks colouring delicately, she became aware of Josephine's curious glance. 'Do you know where my—my husband has gone, Josephine?'

'Gone to see Mr Turner, I think.'

As Emma pondered this slowly, wondering why it should make her feel uneasy, Josephine shrugged her magnificent shoulders. 'I hope you don't think I'm not stirring myself plenty today, Mrs Rick, but the boss he says something about there only being you for lunch. Everyone else he's taking back to Barbados.'

Back to Barbados? Emma went cold all over with stunned surprise. So all along Rick must have intended leaving her. He was returning to Barbados alone, leaving her here, possibly until their divorce was through. She was to be a prisoner, condemned to beautiful but solitary confinement. Her face white, she stumbled to her feet. With a murmured excuse for Josephine, she made for the beach.

It was a glorious morning, the scenery looking so crisp and fresh as to be good enough to eat. Emma, for once, failed to notice, although she was subconsciously aware of the reviving quality of the air as she gulped down great mouthfuls of it. Feeling ill, she wandered dejectedly, blindly watching the huge rollers, the gaily coloured birds. She tried not to think of yesterday, when she had gone sailing with Dan and Rick.

If only Rick hadn't made love to her. Or pretended, this morning, his feelings towards her were changing. He must have decided that this was the only way to keep her calm until after he had gone. Yet she couldn't conceive anyone acting so cruelly. Eventually she gave up trying to make sense of it and, her small face bleak with unhappiness, she returned to the house. It was after twelve. Perhaps by now everyone would be gone. Feverishly she hoped so. If not, then she must pretend she didn't care. There was no other way.

She went into the lounge just a few minutes before Rick arrived. Puzzled to find the two girls still there, Emma kept her face blank. It wasn't easy, but she managed. Both Veronica and Gail had drinks in their hands, but while Gail merely looked bored and indifferent, Veronica was obviously agitated.

'Where on earth have you been?' she asked Emma angrily, when she came in alone.

Emma, feeling startled by Veronica's unconcealed anger, wondered in some bewilderment if her absence had something to do with them still being here. Had Rick, with his fondness for watching her squirm, insisted on waiting to say goodbye? 'I've been down on the beach,' she said. 'Have you been looking for me?'

Contemptuously Veronica shook her head. 'Have you seen anything of Rick?' she demanded.

'Not since earlier this morning,' Emma replied stoically, thinking it better to keep her sentences short, for fear she broke down—or said something she might regret.

Gail glanced curiously at Veronica's disturbed face. 'Josephine says we're going home, Veronica. Rick left orders that we were to be ready to leave.'

Veronica glared at her. 'You don't have to keep repeating it! I'll be glad to leave, providing Rick's coming too. I hate this damned island anyway.'

'I'm not going anywhere,' Rick's drawling voice came from the doorway, spinning them all around. 'Wherever did you get that idea from, Veronica?'

As Emma stared at him blankly, she heard Veronica exclaim triumphantly, 'You ought to sack that old bag in the kitchen, darling. I knew she was just talking through her hat!'

'No, she wasn't,' Rick snapped coldly. Ignoring Veronica, he crossed to Emma's side, frowning down on her pale face. 'I don't know what's been going on, Emma, but I hope you haven't been alarmed.'

Aware that Rick's solicitude wasn't pleasing Veronica, Emma shook her head. Despite the gentleness in Rick's voice she wasn't quite sure what to make of it. He said he wasn't going, but everything that had happened this morning seemed to contradict him. Was he, for some reason, trying to deceive both herself and Veronica?

She was startled to find his arm going around her as he spoke to Veronica and his sister. 'I've spent the morning arranging things with Larry Turner. There's been a lot to get through, it took longer than I thought it would. To cut a long story short, he's going to Barbados on three weeks' leave. You two are going back with him while Emma and I remain here.'

'You and Emma!' Veronica's voice was suddenly incredulous. 'But why, Rick? You can't be serious?'

'Why not?' He was coldly arrogant. 'We do happen to be married.'

'But what about me?' Veronica asked shrilly. 'You've led me to expect . . .'

'What?' he prompted, his eyes narrowing scornfully, while the arm around Emma tightened. 'I can't think of even one occasion when I might have led you to expect anything, Veronica.'

'Maybe not,' she was forced to agree, 'but I thought—well, everyone did, even when you were engaged to that other girl—that you really loved me.' Her voice rose belligerently. 'Rita was sure of it!'

'People are apt to see only what they want to see, and half the time they aren't even sure what that is,' Rick rejoined dryly. As she opened her mouth to protest, he continued levelly, 'We understand each other well enough, Veronica. We've certainly never had an affair—or even pretended to care for each other.'

'Well, you can't care for her!' Veronica's face, as she

glared at Emma, was ugly with hatred and fury. She couldn't stand being spurned, especially in public, and never appreciated the truth. If Rick hadn't held Emma so closely, her fury was such that it was clear to all she would liked to have clawed her apart. 'You just can't care for that low creature!' she gasped.

'I see no point in continuing this discussion,' he snapped, with a coldness which appeared to take the last of Veronica's self-control.

'You're a liar!' she shrieked. 'Rick, how can you stay with her when you don't even trust her? You might be infatuated, but you once told me you didn't believe in love without trust. You said so yourself.'

Rick's voice hardened and his eyes contained ice. 'I presume you're referring to the time when your brother saw himself stepping into my shoes? That episode is over and done with, and you won't mention it again,'

Far from shutting her up, as he obviously intended, Rick's contempt only appeared to goad Veronica to greater lengths. 'I had only to whisper in your ear, the evening you returned from Canada, that Emma was in the garden with Miles, for you to look absolutely murderous. You believed the worst straight away. Then,' she rushed on furiously, as Rick turned pale, 'later, upstairs, you believed she'd accepted a valuable bracelet from Miles.'

'How did you know that?' Rick's deceptively even tones didn't fool Emma. She sensed his mounting anger and shivered. Veronica must have been vaguely aware of it too, as she faltered, not replying to Rick's question. After a brief moment he went on, 'Okay, Veronica, although I hope never to see you again, you do have a point. It's nothing, however, that Emma and I can't sort out. Now Dan is waiting to take you to the jetty. I don't want to throw you out, but would you please leave while we say goodbye to Gail?'

'That bracelet——' Veronica's brief silence was short-lived. Emma could see that Rick's abrupt dismissal had enraged her further and she was resolved not to leave until he heard everything she had to say. 'That bracelet,' she reiterated sharply. 'Didn't you ever discover it was I who put it in Emma's room? You threw it back at Miles and nearly killed him, and you threw your precious Emma out because you believed she was having an affair with him. You thought she'd hidden the bracelet in her drawer while all the time it was I who'd put it there.'

Rick's voice was terse with fury. 'You—My God!'

'Yes!' Veronica assured him defiantly. 'And I managed to be outside her bedroom door when you found it and accused her of accepting presents from her lover. If you'd loved her you wouldn't have doubted when she tried to tell you she was innocent. You would have realised, as well, that she's too besotted with you to see any other man.'

Rick's voice softened but, to Emma's ears, seemed all the more deadly for that. 'I could break your neck, Veronica. Or worse!'

Emma didn't wait to hear more. Tearing herself from Rick's arms, she took no notice of his terse exclamation as she ran from the room. Through a blur she saw Veronica throw herself hysterically in his path as he made to follow her. She could only feel thankful that something had stopped him.

She had several minutes' start and made for the southern shore of the island, where there were many hidden coves. These she had discovered on one of her many lonely rambles, before Rick came. She didn't really imagine he would rush after her—not after he'd had a moment to cool down. Then, when he realised the truth of what Veronica had been saying, he might leave with her. If he didn't—Emma sighed; well, at least she would have time to pull herself together and decide what to do. Sometimes the island fishermen left their boats unattended. She might escape Rick forever if she could find one of those.

Emma, being young and supple, ran swiftly, a fury of despair driving her on. Veronica was right: Rick had never trusted her. He had only pretended he cared for her. He had obviously developed, as men sometimes did for a woman, a fleeting lust for her, but once this had been assuaged he would have cast her out—as he had done all the others. Bitterly she ran on while reflecting on this, tears streaming down her hot cheeks.

Eventually arriving at a cove which she considered sufficiently hidden, she threw herself down exhausted in some long grass. She must have cried herself to sleep, and when she woke she was stiff and sore and her bed of grass wasn't so comfortable any more.

Frowning, she lay staring up at the sky. Unhappily, as her first surge of indignation died down, she knew she must go back to the house. Escaping in a fishing boat was not for her. Wryly she sighed over her own foolishness. She couldn't, however, contemplate facing Rick yet. Despondently she wondered what she would find to say to him, if he was still on the island. Instead of thinking things out she had simply gone to sleep. Now she felt angry for having wasted so much time.

Hazily her mind clouded again as her thoughts returned painfully to the amazing conversation between Rick and Veronica. What a crazy sequence of events had been uncovered! Veronica must indeed have been crazy to have acted as she had done. But at least she had revealed Rick's weak spot, a flaw in his character, his lack of trust.

Yet—Emma paused uncertainly, as she scrubbed away another flood of tears. In his shoes, what would she have done? Hadn't she suspected him of having an affair with Veronica when apparently he had not? With both Rick and herself, mightn't it have been a case, not so much of lack of trust as lack of faith in their own ability to hold on to something precious? If she had found something belonging to another girl—no, an expensive present from another girl in Rick's room—might not she, too, have jumped to the wrong conclusions? Rick had been very angry about Miles's bracelet, but she realised now that he had had every reason to be, for hadn't the planted evidence been very convincing?

Feeling suddenly very small and humble, Emma rose to her feet and began walking quickly back the way she had come. If Rick was still on the island she must find him and apologise for running away. There were other things she must apologise for too, if he would listen. That he mightn't be prepared to frightened her and caused her feet to stumble.

Such was her state of nervous uncertainty that she felt like turning and running again when she saw Rick coming towards her. He was riding a horse. So was Dan, who was following him. When Rick spotted her he exchanged a quick word with Dan who immediately rode off in another direction.

Cantering up to her, Rick slid to the ground. He looked grim and tense as he let go of his reins to grasp Emma's shoulders. He was still wearing the thin shirt and cotton trousers he had had on before lunch and the tall strength of his body seemed like a haven after a storm.

He was pale, Emma noticed, but otherwise appeared to be exercising a tight self-control. It was hard to tell whether he was angry or not. She sensed he was concerned, but then he was the kind of man who might worry over the least of his huge work-force, should one of them become missing.

When it did come, his voice was as grim as his face. 'Where on earth have you been, Emma? I was beginning to think you must have met with an accident!'

She found it difficult to meet the blaze of anger in his

eyes. Scuffing her toe in the sand, she bent her head miserably. 'I'm sorry.'

A muscle jerked at the side of Rick's mouth. 'God— you just seemed to disappear!'

Swallowing a lump in her throat, she asked inadequately, 'Where are the others?'

'If you mean Gail and Larry, they're on their way back to Barbados with Veronica.'

'Veronica?'

'Don't talk about her, Emma, please.'

Hearing the contempt in her voice, she made no further attempt to. 'Why was Dan with you?' she asked instead.

'We organised a search party when I failed to find you. I couldn't take any chances.'

Emma swayed, as remorse and reaction hit her badly. 'I'm sorry, Rick. I know I shouldn't have ran off as I did, but it has helped to clear my—my head.'

'I wish it had done me as much good,' he snapped. 'I've been half out of my mind looking for you, but I'm not altogether convinced it's done you much good either. You look about ready to drop.'

'I'm quite all right, Rick, really.' But before she could say anything more he had tossed her on the horse and swung himself up behind her.

'Home, my girl,' he commanded, 'and a hot bath. Then we'll talk, and there won't be any putting off this time.'

'I've slept,' she protested weakly.

'In sand and grass and tears,' he retorted grimly, his arms tightening until flames began licking through her. 'I've rarely seen your face so white, but that's something I hope to alter.'

Josephine had a hot bath already run, for Dan had raced back and told her Emma had been found. She was anxious to see to Emma herself, but Rick dismissed her. He told her to leave their dinner and go home. Suddenly Josephine was all smiles as she bade them both goodnight.

She had laid a cold buffet in the dining-room. There was only the soup to heat and coffee to make, she said innocently, if they ever got down again.

Rick tested the water, himself, before ordering Emma to get undressed and get in. He was so grim that she understood, without him having to put it in words, that if she didn't obey immediately he would do it for her. She heard the shower running next door and when, ten minutes later, she went into the bedroom, she found him there, waiting for her.

They were both wearing short robes. 'We should be getting dressed, shouldn't we?' she faltered, suddenly self-conscious.

'Come here,' he said, so forcibly that she dared not disobey.

He was sitting on the side of the bed and as she approached he jerked her down beside him. 'You wanted to talk, Rick,' she reminded him hastily, as something in his eyes almost stopped her breath.

'Later, honey.' He pulled her against him with a sudden urgency which made her tremble as his mouth sought hers with demanding pressure. As his hand cupped her chin she was unable to move. Heat flooded them both and he pushed her back on the bed, his hard body pinning hers down. Fiercely he continued kissing her while she sighed against his lips and pressed helplessly closer.

'I want you so damn much,' he groaned, his eyes aflame as his gaze flickered over her parted robe, and her fingertips explored the roughness of his broad chest. 'I'm not sure I could think straight, let alone talk sensibly about anything.'

Emma had no desire to talk herself. In only moments Rick had aroused her to incredible heights, and she was taking an intense pleasure in her own tentative discoveries. When he had made love to her before she had barely been allowed time. Now it was different—or so she thought, until his mouth closed passionately over hers and her heart leaped wildly in response.

'Rick . . .' she faltered, as he gasped, 'please think clearly about this. I couldn't bear it if you left me again afterwards. After you'd gone, last time, you don't know how I felt . . .'

'You mean the first time?' Tenderly he withdrew a little, his hand caressing her hot cheeks. Gently he thrust the heavy hair off her face, so he might see her better. 'My little love, you must have guessed why I didn't touch you again. I thought—and you let me believe—you were experienced, and I was way beyond stopping when I realised I was the first. Heaven help me, I tried, but it was no use. I'd never been at the mercy of my emotions like that before!' He paused, sighing ruefully. 'Sweetheart, you affect me worse than strong drink.' Then, the teasing curve of his mouth straightening bleakly, he met her suddenly shy eyes. 'I almost went out of my mind. I had to leave you. Why did you let me believe you were Oliver's girl, when you must have known what kind of girl that made you? If I'd had any idea you were absolutely innocent I'd never have married you.'

'That was why I didn't tell you, Rick,' she whispered. 'I wanted to escape from the farm and that seemed the only chance I was likely to get. If I'd told you I'd never even been out with a man before, you wouldn't have taken me away. I had to make a quick decision, but I felt fairly safe when you said it would just be a marriage of convenience. I didn't count on falling in love with you, though.'

His head jerked up. 'Say that again,' he demanded hoarsely. When she obliged, he said thickly, 'I've been a brute, darling. I don't deserve your love, but, for what it's worth, I love you, too. Desperately . . .'

'I didn't want to love you,' she confessed, as his arms tightened about her half naked body. 'I tried to fight it.'

His dark brows rose wryly. 'Not nearly so much as I did, I guess.'

'I tried not to think of how I felt when you kissed me,' she murmured huskily.

With a smothered exclamation he began kissing her again until within the circle of his arms she started to tremble with emotion and need. 'Oh, my love,' Rick muttered against her mouth, 'you weren't the only one. You made me angrier than I could ever remember being before. I often felt quite savage just looking at you. I thought that was behind the totally unreal sensations I felt when I kissed you. After my last visit to the farm, during the whole of the ten days I was away, this strange anger, as I chose to call it, obsessed me to the exclusion of everything else. I hated even to think of Rex Oliver.'

'You really were convinced he was my—my lover?'

'I was,' Rick confessed. 'I'm afraid I never questioned what you and Blanche told me. I think I'd reached the age when I imagined I had few illusions left about women. I met Blanche and was momentarily attracted, but when I decided to marry her it was with my eyes wide open. I was aware that she loved me no more than I loved her. I wanted a son and heir while she wanted money. It seemed to me, after we'd supplied each other's needs, that we could go our separate ways without regret. Now I don't believe she would have supplied me with anything. But I was so arrogant that if she'd married me I believe I would have deserved everything I got.'

His mouth quirked in self-derision. 'When I returned from Australia, expecting to find her meekly waiting for me, my male ego suffered a considerable blow on discovering she was in Paris with Oliver. I thought I'd found in you—such a plain little thing—the perfect means of revenge. But,' he groaned thickly against Emma's breast, 'even before we were married I was beginning to realise I'd had it. I was lost before I even started. You were able to make my pulse race in a way I'd never experienced with Blanche or any other woman.'

'You didn't appear to be falling in love with me,' Emma faltered.

'I was fighting it, darling,' his mouth returned to hers and he muttered against it. 'You must have heard how a doomed man invariably struggles! But it was in Barbados that I really panicked.' Ironically he smiled as his hand smoothed her shoulder. 'No woman, certainly not an un-fledged girl, was going to take me over! I ran, thinking it was just a case of putting a little distance between us, but instead of curing me, every day away from you only made my longing worse. When I returned I was almost prepared to go down on my knees and beg, but when I found two men fighting over you I was consumed by a jealous rage. There seemed significant differences, too, in both your face and figure. That bracelet, which I was told Miles had given you, was the last straw.'

It was then that Emma told him about her father's death, and how the subsequent hard years on the farm had made her thin. That was how the weeks of idleness and good food on Barbados had made such a difference. 'I was just getting back my confidence and looks when you arrived and shattered everything,' she sighed. 'Miles and Ben might believe they're fond of me, but I don't think they care all that much.'

'You'd be surprised,' Rick rejoined curtly, his face dark-ening. 'I'm sorry, my darling, that I treated you as I did, but everything seemed so wrong somehow. And when I found that damned bracelet I felt like murder! When Veronica confessed this morning that she'd put it in your drawer, it was all I could do to keep my hands off her.'

'She must have taken it from Miles's car.' Emma frowned, trying to remember. 'Unfortunately she came across us in the shop, just as Miles was attempting to persuade me to have it. When I refused she said something

which annoyed him and he slipped it in his pocket.'
Nervously Emma hesitated, as her mind dwelt unhappily
on that distressing afternoon. 'I felt so mixed up and guilty
about Miles that I agreed to have tea with him, in order
to make sure he understood there could never be anything
between us. He must have left the bracelet in the car and
when Veronica arrived at the house shortly afterwards
she must have seen it and taken it. Miles must have
thought I had. I remember he gave me a slightly puzzled
glance. I believe now that was why he acted as he did at
Rita's party. He'd obviously decided I'd changed my
mind about him.'

Rick said quietly, his breath warm on her pale face,
'Last night, while you slept and I held you, I suddenly
knew you weren't guilty of any of the crimes I'd accused
you of. That doesn't excuse me for doubting you in the
first place, but I'm afraid I was blind with jealousy, my
darling.'

'I shouldn't have gone out with Miles even once, Rick,'
she replied ruefully. 'I was using him, I think, in order to
forget you, but I never pretended I felt anything but
friendship for him.'

'I'm glad.' Rick's hand tightened possessively over her
shoulder. 'There have been other women in my life, but
none since I met you. Veronica was always running to me
with her problems. Occasionally I took her somewhere
for dinner to help sort them out, but there was never
anything romantic about it. To me she was more like a
sister—an irritating one at that.'

'I was so miserable while you were away,' Emma confessed bleakly. 'I think I was ready to believe you loved
anyone but me. And then you talked of getting a
divorce!'

'That being my original line, I felt I had to stick to it.'
He kissed her firmly, with a hint of his old arrogance,
then muttered huskily, 'There won't be any more talk of

divorce, now or ever. You're mine until eternity—and afterwards. I hope you understand?'

Emma felt fire spreading through her rapidly as his mouth slid to her throat and then the warm curve of her breast. As her arms tightened convulsively around his neck, Rick raised his head and looked at her, his eyes very dark and demanding. She swallowed, unable to speak, but her lips parted. With a muttered groan, his control went and he began kissing her until her passion rose to meet his. Later, when he had gasped out his pleasure against her shuddering, satisfied body, he assured her tensely that he would never let her go.

Holding her possessively close, he studied her dewy young face, on which the aftermath of their loving had left a soft glow. 'We have at least three weeks here,' his voice held tender menace. 'I hope you're prepared to love me a lot?'

'Three weeks?' Emma nodded contentedly, unable to think of anything she'd like better.

'Yes,' Rick growled, with another kiss. 'Larry Turner will stay on Barbados until Gail decides whether they're really made for each other or not. I rather think she'll go to Australia with Rita to keep house for Ben. After they've gone we go back to live at Coral House. I made enquiries, by the way,' he added, 'about your aunt in England. I learnt that the farm has been sold and she's gone to live with her sister. So you have nothing left to worry about.'

'Only you,' Emma teased, meeting his passionate gaze, while her heart leapt with a warm excitement as Rick outlined the course of their life together. He must care for her a lot to have dealt so firmly with his stepmother and bothered to find out what had happened to Aunt Hilda.

'I love you,' she whispered fervently, her hands caressing his face, 'and I love this island. I don't think I shall ever want to leave it.'

'We'll return often,' he promised softly, as her exploring fingers slid to his broad shoulders. 'You're tormenting me, young woman!' he groaned thickly.

'Oh, darling,' she breathed, drawing him down to her, every nerve tingling at his nearness and the naked flames in his eyes.

'I'm lost,' he gasped. 'So completely enslaved, I can't even fight any more.'

'Why try?' Emma whispered shamelessly, as he began telling her how much he loved her, while his hand went out silently to douse the light.

A WORD ABOUT THE AUTHOR

Margaret Pargeter was born in the quiet Northumbrian Valley, in the extreme northeast of England, where she lives today.

When did she first feel an urge to write? "Truthfully, I can't recall," she admits. "It must have been during my early teens. I remember carrying a notebook in my pocket, and while milking cows I would often take a break to scribble something down."

The jottings developed into short stories, and Margaret's first break came several years after she had married. Her husband talked her into entering a writing contest, and her work caught the eye of an editor, who asked her to write serial stories. From there she went on to complete her first romance novel, *Winds from the Sea* (Romance #1899).

Among the author's many blessings, which she likes to keep counting, is the "pleasure I get from knowing that people enjoy reading my books. And," she adds, "I hope they long continue to do so."

Take these
4 best-selling novels
FREE

Yes! Four sophisticated, contemporary love stories by four world-famous authors of romance FREE, as your introduction to the Harlequin Presents subscription plan. Thrill to **Anne Mather**'s passionate story BORN OUT OF LOVE, set in the Caribbean.... Travel to darkest Africa in **Violet Winspear**'s TIME OF THE TEMPTRESS....Let **Charlotte Lamb** take you to the fascinating world of London's Fleet Street in MAN'S WORLD .... Discover beautiful Greece in **Sally Wentworth**'s moving romance SAY HELLO TO YESTERDAY.

Harlequin Presents...

The very finest in romance fiction

Join the millions of avid Harlequin readers all over the world who delight in the magic of a really exciting novel. EIGHT great NEW titles published EACH MONTH! Each month you will get to know exciting, interesting, true-to-life people .... You'll be swept to distant lands you've dreamed of visiting .... Intrigue, adventure, romance, and the destiny of many lives will thrill you through each Harlequin Presents novel.

Get all the latest books before they're sold out!
As a Harlequin subscriber you actually receive your personal copies of the latest Presents novels immediately after they come off the press, so you're sure of getting all 8 each month.

Cancel your subscription whenever you wish!
You don't have to buy any minimum number of books. Whenever you decide to stop your subscription just let us know and we'll cancel all further shipments.